The Trust Heritage

The Strings of Past Can Shake the Future

S. P. Nayak

Ukiyoto Publishing

All global publishing rights are held by

Ukiyoto Publishing

Published in 2023

Content Copyright © S. P. Nayak

ISBN 9789360164522

All rights reserved.
No part of this publication may be reproduced, transmitted, or stored in a retrieval system, in any form by any means, electronic, mechanical, photocopying, recording or otherwise, without the prior permission of the publisher.

The moral rights of the author have been asserted.

This is a work of fiction. Names, characters, businesses, places, events, locales, and incidents are either the products of the author's imagination or used in a fictitious manner. Any resemblance to actual persons, living or dead, or actual events is purely coincidental.

This book is sold subject to the condition that it shall not by way of trade or otherwise, be lent, resold, hired out or otherwise circulated, without the publisher's prior consent, in any form of binding or cover other than that in which it is published.

www.ukiyoto.com

Dedication

In the Loving Memory of
My Father
Late Pt. Shri Ram Sewak Nayak

Grandparents
Late Pt. Shri Ram Dayal–Smt. Kanchan Nayak

Uncles
Late Pt. Shri Rameshwar Prasad Nayak
Late Pt. Shri Suresh Prasad Nayak

&

Father-in-Law
Late Dr. H. N. Mishra

Acknowledgements

I would like to express my indebtedness to the unconditional love and affection showered by my mother **Mrs. Ramdevi Nayak** whose treasure of blessings never goes out of supply, my wife **Rolly** and daughter **Mauli** whose love has ever been a source of inspiration, my sisters, brothers-in-law and nephews who have always supported me, and my niece **Shefali** who infused me with the spirit of enthusiasm.

I would also like to thank **Ukiyoto Publishing** for showing trust in my work. The words of appreciation enhance the confidence of the author, while suggestions enable him to improve the quality. I would also like to express my thankfulness to **Dr. Yashwant Mishra** for his continuous support during the work. Apart from these names, there are many who have directly or indirectly contributed to the evolution of this work. I would like to express my gratitude to every member of my extended family and the staff of my workplace, **Govt. Polytechnic College, Nowgong**.

And last but not the least, I consider myself to be fortunate to be born in the Bundelkhand Region, which holds a prosperous heritage of the great Indian Cultural Rainbow. Nowgong town has witnessed various events of history during the Pre and Post-Independence era and has remained a central place holding the crowning glory throughout the chronology of events, from being the headquarters of Bundelkhand agency to the capital of a state. I have spent more than a decade in the town, which can be truly called the Consciousness Capital of Bundelkhand. I would like to thank the people of the town who have toiled hard to maintain the grandeur and the unique vigour that epitomise the spirit of the town.

Contents

The Genesis	1
The Prelude	7
The Ripple	12
The Chimera	15
The Revelation	18
The Reconnaissance	34
The Probe	39
Exploring the Lost Ends	43
Facing the Ferals	48
The Redeemer	52
Cleaning the Cobwebs	61
Breezing in the Boot Camp	65
The Faux Pas	72
The Stepping Stones	74
A Saviour in the Maze	78
The Alchemist	86
Taming the Nemesis	97
Getting to the Oasis	105
The Glory of the Past	115
Bidding Adieu	119
The Retreat	122
Reaching the Terminus	124
The Epiphany	126
About the Author	*136*

The Genesis

Bhaskar sat up suddenly and held his head in both hands. His heart was pounding so hard that he could feel it striking his ribs. He kept still for a while and then turned his head towards the clock, which showed quarter to five in the morning.

He had had the same dream again. He lay back slowly and recalled it. As soon as he closed his eyes, the train of thoughts started. The whole dream experience started to flash again. He remembered everything clearly and lucidly. He was standing in complete darkness, until a flare of light flickered somewhere on the horizon, which revealed a silhouette of a big structure with three rising towers with domes and peaks. The middle tower was higher than the other two towers. He realised that he was in the backyard of the building and the darkness enveloped him again. Then, he noticed a gleam of light peeping from the floor just ahead of him. He moved towards it and found an opening with a stairway. He went downstairs and reached a vault-like structure made of glittering gold. The place had numerous wooden boxes filled with gold ingots. As soon as he picked up an ingot, he felt a jolt and the whole vault started to sink down. He rushed upstairs and reached the landing stair but realised that the opening was far away from him, and the distance was increasing gradually. He wanted to scream when the loud sound of a conch shell echoed all around. An intense blaze of light emerged at the entrance and faded gradually. In the centre of the glimmer, a figure appeared with a scroll in his hand. He identified the figure as his grandfather. He shouted with joy "Dada Ji!" He realised that his grandfather was about to say something and only then, he woke up. The same thing happened this time too.

Bhaskar, a young Adonis aged around twenty-four, was born in a small village, but his father arranged his schooling at a renowned boarding school. He had recently completed his post-graduation acclaiming the Gold Medal for outstanding performance. He had always been a meritorious student, and his talent received admiration from every acquaintance. He was now preparing for competitive exams to get a respectable government job. However, he wanted to do something innovative and pursue his career as a writer, but he knew well that his talent and intelligence would be considered useless if he did not get a good job.

He hailed from a middle-class Brahmin family of a village in the Bundelkhand region of Central India. His father was a government school teacher who had retired recently, and his mother was a housewife. His family was a typical Brahmin family, having deep-rooted faith in religion and religious practices. They held the ideology, norms and values of Hinduism, and the spirit of the rural Indian community. The people of this area firmly believed in the notion that the ultimate obligation of every educated individual was to get a good government job, failing which the entire education was futile.

There was a popular saying in the area that *"Education takes a kid away, either from home or from fields."* The saying expressed that education would either make one relocate somewhere away from home, or if, by chance, one stays at home, he would remain useless for agricultural work. So, in order to keep one's kids home, keep them away from education. The decision to pursue education can be called justified only if it leads to a lucrative government job.

Bhaskar knew well that every jobless year would aggravate the intensity of the questions being raised about his abilities, and a few years later his brilliance would be considered as false propaganda if he couldn't get a good job. Despite having a clear understanding of his competence and the area of his interest, he dared not deviate from the notion as he was aware of the financial status of his family and the aspirations of his father. He knew that his father had spent far beyond his financial capabilities to provide him with quality education. Thus, the only way he could really help him was to help him financially.

When he returned to normalcy, a series of questions started to strike his mind. Bhaskar was quite aware that dreams are a normal activity, but its recurrence aroused numerous questions in his mind. Bhaskar was around eight years old when his grandfather passed away and after sixteen years, his grandfather's appearance in his dream seemed a little strange to him. "Had his portrait not been displayed in the drawing room, I might not have even remembered his face," he said to himself.

The recurrence of the dream compelled him to shun his insouciance on the matter. He was a little concerned about the dream and started to speculate about the reasons. He experienced multiple thoughts coming to him and most of them were dreary. All the horror, paranormal and psycho-thriller movies and novels he had watched or read started to appear before him. "Is some evil spirit showing its influence? Is this a paranormal haunting? Is this oneirophrenia? Am I a patient of dementia? Am I suffering from some dissociative disorder?" He got scared.

He gathered all his rational thoughts to dominate the scary ideas plaguing his mind and heart. He repeated to himself that dreams are merely a result of unfiltered information processed by the brain.

Then, he thought of sharing this experience with his father. He tried to envision the possible reactions of his father and he was reminded of the incident that occurred yesterday. The whole incident started to appear before him.

Bhaskar was very excited and happy. Holding a letter in his hand, he ran to his father and said, "Papa, my article has been accepted in the *Times of India*. It will be published next week. I just received this letter sent by the editor of the newspaper through post. He wrote that he liked my article very much and had not suggested even a single correction. I had heard that this newspaper accepts articles after rigorous quality checks at multiple stages, but my very first article got accepted." Bhaskar said it all in one breath.

Bhaskar's happiness knew no bounds, but Bhaskar's father didn't seem happy. He forced a smile on his face and said, "Good." Father's cold reaction made his enthusiasm evaporate.

Father sensed his state of mind and, in a restrained voice, said, "Son, you will get enough time throughout your life to write articles. But this golden time will never come back. Now leave all these useless time killers and focus on shaping your career. Hardly four months are left for the Civil Services exam. Once you crack the exam, life will improve—yours as well as ours. You know very well about our financial hardships. How did I incur the expenses of your education in a metro? How did I manage the expenses of the marriage of your elder sisters, and before that, the marriage of my younger sisters and the education of two younger brothers? These events demanded huge expenses, and the only source of income that I had was the salary of a school teacher. My father left no property, no money. I inherited only piles of books from my father. I do not have any property or bank balance. Still, an amount of about thirteen lakhs is outstanding of the personal and auto loans which I borrowed for the marriage of your sister. This is when

I paid every penny that I received as my retirement benefits, against my dues. Only I know how I am managing all this with the small amount I receive as my pension. It's God's mercy that there is a provision for pension, so the condition of the family has not gone public." He paused for a while.

He continued, "Had the pension not been there, we would have starved. So, it is expected from you that you grab a job that offers power and money. This is the only way to secure your future and ease our last days. Have you ever looked at your mother? In forty years, I could not buy gold bangles for her. Your mother, too, strangled all her desires. Don't you think that, in such a situation, you should prefer cracking the exam to writing articles? The key to our happiness lies in your performance in the exam. Poverty is a black hole that devours one's volition, hobbies and desires. Had we been an affluent family, you could've spent your life seeking your satisfaction by writing articles and stories, but our family cannot afford that."

Father's long speech transported Bhaskar to the ground from cloud nine. He walked back to his room with heavy steps. He reached his room and sat on his study chair. The envelope that contained the letter from the editor of the newspaper regarding acceptance of his article for publication was still lying on the table.

He tore the envelope and the letter into small pieces and threw them into the bin. He was panting due to frustration, anger and gloom. Suddenly, his eyes rested on the pile of books on his table and his father's exhortation about grandfather's bequest started echoing in his ears, *"I inherited only piles of books from my father."*

He relived the whole incident again and the replay of the conversation with his father filled him again with distress and gloomy annoyance. He realized that sharing the dream experience with his father might result in another similar incident. So, he rejected the idea of sharing the dream with his parents. He continued to brood until he got the voice of his mother, "Bhaskar, get up, it is already seven o'clock! Tea is ready." His mother's voice transported him to the real world, and he realised that he had been tangled in a web of thoughts for more than two hours.

The Prelude

Bhaskar didn't have any plans for seeking any specific thing from his grandfather's room, but despite having no clear motive, he felt an urge to go there. He opened the door and entered the room. He looked all around. The floor, the walls and the roof were clean as the room was being cleaned regularly and whitewashed every Diwali. He experienced a kind of vellichor in the room as it was filled with books all over. The room had many built-in shelves made in a set of three within the thirty-inch-thick walls. One set of shelves was framed with wooden panels and a tiny brass lock was hanging on the staple of a robust hasp.

The open shelves, the loft and racks were stuffed with books of varied sizes and their yellowish colour itself was expressing their age. The books on the shelves were stacked, while the books in the loft were piled. There were some bundles, tied with cloth sheets, placed in the loft along with two wooden boxes. He was surprised that the boxes were almost similar to the boxes that appeared in his dream. He stared at the boxes for a long time and then realised that almost all the wooden boxes appeared similar and thus it was not a potent point to think upon.

There was a picture of Lord Vishnu and Goddess Laxmi, with the caption "Shri Laxmi Narayan" hanging on a wall. The dust deposits on the picture and books conveyed that the room was not in use and was opened only for the cleaning ritual every alternate day. Bhaskar reached near a shelf and realised that these shelves had remained untouched since the demise of his grandfather, and no one had ever taken any interest even in looking at the books. He, too, had entered this room after years.

He drew books one by one from the stacks and started flipping through the pages. After browsing through the books of a few stacks, he apprehended that the books were related either to Astrology or to Vedic Mathematics. Most of the books were not comprehensible to him as they were in Sanskrit. Few books were so old that the pages crumbled just in an attempt of flipping. Then, he moved to the next shelf and started browsing the books from a new stack. He kept on browsing the books and after scouring the shelf, he realised that this collection was dedicated to Ayurveda, as he himself was familiar with the names of a few titles and authors.

Suddenly, his father entered the room and asked him, "Are you looking for something, son?"

"No, not actually, I am trying to get an insight into the subjects Dada Ji used to learn," Bhaskar answered after quickly managing a flurry.

A smile appeared on his father's face and then disappeared. He walked to Bhaskar, put a hand on his shoulder and said, "Yes, Your Dada Ji was a great scholar, but he remained a learner till his last breath, even though he was a master in every area of his practice. People used to call him 'Acharya Ji.' He was a 'Raśvaidya Shastri'[1] with exceptional knowledge of Ayurveda and Vedic Chemistry, a brilliant astrologer, a genius mathematician and a great scholar of Sanskrit. He attained such a high status in these fields that the most renowned names of his time used to come to him, to take his opinion on complex issues. He was addressed as 'Vaidya Ratnakara'[2] by other scholars. He practised Ayurvedic Medicine as a profession. He relinquished fame and name throughout his life and adopted

---

[1] *A master practitioner of the drugs of metals/minerals origin in Ayurveda*
[2] *An honorary title given to an Ayurvedic practitioner for extraordinary contribution in the field*

all measures to keep away from the limelight. His aim was to acquire knowledge only. He didn't have any fascination for wealth or for any material attainment. He was very popular as a Vaidya within the area of nearby villages where he would commute to visit patients. Few people believe that he was an Alchemist."

Bhaskar exclaimed with surprise, "Alchemist! Papa, did you say Alchemist?"

Father gave a dry smile and said, "Yes, many people believed that he was an Alchemist."

Bhaskar's face reflected the feelings of confusion and strangeness. He said, "What is meant by the belief of people? Didn't you know? Being an Alchemist is the rarest of the rare achievements."

Father's face expressed a tinge of melancholy, and all the efforts to cover those feelings with a smile turned useless. He said, "I do think that he was an Alchemist. For a man of his intellectual and spiritual stature, having profound knowledge of Alchemy was no surprise. But he himself neither accepted it nor denied it."

A mixed expression of surprise and joy flashed on Bhaskar's face. He asked his father, "Papa, why have you not tried to learn these things from him?"

Bhaskar's question brought again a tinge of distress and misery into his expressions. He said in a low voice, "I was the eldest of three brothers and two sisters, so, including my grandmother and my parents, we were a family of eight. There was only one financial source to meet the needs of the family, and that was my father's practice of Ayurvedic Medicine. A large share of his earnings was spent on the purchase of material required for his Ayurvedic research and on the charity of the students he used to teach. The amount left for us was hardly enough to meet our both ends. So, I realised early in my life that I had to choose a different profession to provide basic amenities to my younger brothers and arrange for the wedding of my sisters. Often, my father used to rebuke me for not taking interest in learning Ayurveda. But I had realized that practising Ayurveda cannot fulfil the basic needs of a family, especially in this area with poverty-ridden masses. I was seven years old when the country got independence. But for us, nothing changed, and the Jagir system remained in force for more than three decades. I decided to go for formal school education in a government school. At that time, our village had only a primary school, and the nearest middle school was eleven miles away. It meant that I had to get a hostel facility there. The cost of the boarding facility and canteen charges may seem negligible today, but it was a great challenge to me. The son of the then titular ruler of this area was my classmate. He turned into a very good friend of mine. He was from such an affluent family that his daily pocket money was more than double the amount needed for my monthly expenses. I used to help him with his studies, and he used to pay my hostel fee. Despite all the odds, I completed secondary education anyhow and got a government job as a primary teacher. The small amount received as salary was sufficient to provide good education to my younger brothers and make the arrangements for the marriage of my sisters."

He took a deep breath and continued, "I had two choices. Either to follow my father's way of life, that is to attain knowledge and continue the life of destitution, or to earn some money by being mediocre and fulfilling the basic needs of the family. Knowledge cannot satiate hunger and look at the greater irony— it cannot be attained on a hungry stomach." His tone was tinged with regret.

Bhaskar could understand the internal strife that his father was experiencing. He said, "Papa, I am not blaming you or your decision. I know that you have performed all your responsibilities very well. Had anyone been in your place, he would have done the same thing."

Bhaskar paused for a while and then asked, "Had you ever discussed the financial status of the family with him?"

Father said, "He was an altruist. He never felt the need for money and expected his family to adopt a similar way of life. Once, I requested him to stop spending money on his Ayurvedic experiments and on the charity of his disciples so that some money may be saved and accumulated. He laughed first and then agreed that accumulation is very good practice. But he advised me not to think of accumulating money and rather aim at accumulating knowledge." Father was gasping.

He took a pause, controlled his breath and said with a sigh, "Old wounds may get cured but often they keep on giving pain."

Bhaskar realised that it was better to end the conversation for now. So, he said, "It's already half past one, so let's have lunch, mother must be waiting." He followed his father out of the room and latched the door from outside.

The Ripple

Bhaskar was sitting on the chair with his legs stretched on the bed and his eyes were staring at the roof. In a nutshell, his posture was similar to that of a person relaxing on a recliner, but his mind was in no way relaxed. A storm of thoughts was quaking his complete existence as the recurrence of the dream had turned his inner state tumultuous. He couldn't concentrate on anything. He was a rational and well-educated youth, but his thoughts were putting his willpower to an extreme ordeal. He remained in the position for a long time and then, he stood up at once. His facial expressions were indicative of some decision. He went out of his room and walked straight towards his grandfather's room.

Bhaskar opened the door of the room with a little caution to avoid any sound. He looked at the picture of Lord Vishnu and Goddess Laxmi, and then whispered, "God, you are omnipresent and omniscient. Please help me to solve this puzzle as you know everything. I know well that dreams are nothing more than the kaleidoscopic presentation of our thoughts. Had anybody conveyed me a similar situation, I would have suggested that he forget the nonsense and would have laughed at him. Despite being aware of all this, I don't know why I am treating this dream so seriously. I truly want to eradicate all such thoughts from my mind but find myself unable to do so. The dream has turned into a whim. O God, please help me."

Then, he looked all around the room. The almirah was locked and all the books stacked on the shelves were already examined by him. He focused his attention on the loft. He quickly went out of the room and returned with a chair. He stood on the chair and now the objects in the loft were approachable to him. He dragged a bundle, brought it down and placed it on the bench. He tried to dust it off but realised that his action might fill the whole room with dust. So, he started untying the knots of the bundle very carefully. After untying the outer cloth, he found that there was another cloth inside it. He untied it too and gently spread the four corners of those clothes. There were a few books, notebooks and loose pages inside. Apart from this, there was also a small leather bag in it. The leather bag was single-pocketed and contained a very old acknowledgement slip of some registered post. The loose sheets contained handwritten notes with diagrams, perhaps about astronomy, written in Sanskrit. The books, too, were related to astronomy. Bhaskar tied the bundle in the same way as was done earlier and placed it in the loft again.

Then he took one of the wooden boxes down and opened it. The boxes were made of fine teakwood and had a very good build quality. The boxes had beautifully carved edges and "Shri Laxmi Narayan" was mentioned on the front panel in an attractive engraving. The box was filled with open shells of some nut he didn't identify. He picked up a shell, kept it in his pocket and then placed the box back in its place. Next, he opened the other wooden box placed in the loft which contained fourteen large-sized earthen lamps. Bhaskar placed this box back in its place too. There was also a plastic sack filled with clay in the loft. Now, there was nothing left unchecked and unverified in the whole room, except the locked almirah. Bhaskar was extremely disappointed as he didn't notice a single thing that could seem even of little significance.

Bhaskar felt drops of sweat rolling down the back of his ears. The work of lifting and placing all those things for two hours had left him exhausted too. The cocktail of distress and exhaustion resulted in an annoying perplexity, and he felt a kind of frustrating anger. He hit the wall with his fist many times. He came out of the room and rushed to the drawing room.

He stood before the portrait of his grandfather and gazed at the photo. In a state of bewilderment, he started talking to the photo. "Dada Ji, you are smiling. Are you smiling or laughing at my situation? Do you want to make me realise my diminutive cognitive abilities? Are you putting my intellect to a test? I don't have any hesitation to accept that your question is too recondite to be comprehended by my ordinary insight. I cannot understand your language. If you want to tell me something, please make it a little clearer. I can't handle the pressure of this context, which is equally treatable as fact and fiction. I am confused about choosing between faith and reason, between heart and mind, between past and future. I have lost my volition. Will you help me?"

Meanwhile, Bhaskar's mother observed him doing so through the window open towards the courtyard. As she was facing Bhaskar's back, he didn't notice her. She got scared and hastily brought her husband to the scene. They both became very worried and nervous. They could not understand what had suddenly happened to their son.

On the other hand, Bhaskar, who was completely unaware of his parents' situation, kept talking to his grandfather, and then lounged on the sofa with his eyes closed.

The Chimera

Bhaskar's father was sitting on a chair while his mother was sitting on a low-height stool in the courtyard of his house, and Bhaskar was sitting on the third stair of the flight that made the only way to the terrace. Bhaskar felt as if he was a convict appearing before a court of law.

Their abode was a traditional village house with plain rooflines, asymmetrically positioned windows and doors, stairways without rails, a centrally located courtyard with ample area and plain cement flooring. The absence of symmetry in the construction of the house reflected that the house was constructed in parts and in multiple stages.

The faces of the parents were reflecting deep disquietude while Bhaskar was repenting for his misadventure that had resulted in a terrible mess. He had already tried to convince his parents that he was quite well and talking to the portrait was only a gesture of his own frustrating annoyance that he had undergone after the recurrent dream. He didn't have any idea if his revelation of the dream experience would aggravate the situation. But it happened, and Bhaskar witnessed it in the form of rolling tears from his mother's eyes and his father's perturbed face.

Bhaskar's mother was a conservative woman who perfectly represented the class of Indian rural women of the mid twentieth century, who held firm faith in God and followed not only the religious practices but also believed in superstitions, sorcery, magic and spirits. As soon as she learned about Bhaskar's dream, she became very nervous. She closed her eyes and started praying to God with folded hands. "O Lord, protect my son, save him from the evil shadow. If we have made any mistake, then forgive us, and if the mistake is irremissible, then give me the punishment of my son's share."

After listening to his wife's words, Mr. Dixit, being a little irritated, said, "Now your nonsense has started."

But she wasn't ready to listen to anything. She scowled at him and said, "You are considering all this nonsense. You find the name of God nonsense. You do not understand why he is having this dream again and again. Haven't you seen his reaction in the drawing room? It is due to some evil spirit. There are evil spirits who possess the body of a person and make one do everything the spirit wishes."

Mr. Dixit, now in a calm voice, said, "I have also heard those superstitious and irrational stories. You know your father-in-law far better than me. You were his favourite and he treated you as his daughter. You are aware of his spiritual and intellectual level. Even if we consider those fallacious narratives to be true, can any evil spirit be so powerful that it can take his form, even in a dream? Tell me. Can you believe that? So, forget your view of paranormal involvement. Sometimes, something rests so deeply in our unconscious memory that it does not come out easily. Then it appears in a new form in our dreams by mixing with other thoughts of our brain. A psychiatrist may very easily deal with this."

But Mrs. Dixit was not ready to listen to anything, she said, "Whatever you think, I will not wrangle over that, but I will take my son to Cave Baba tomorrow only. Only he can extricate my son from this crisis now. He is miraculous. Out of a crowd of thousands, he calls a person by name, knows his mind even before he can speak. He will understand everything in a moment and once he puts his hand on Bhaskar's head, the whole problem will end."

Mr. Dixit said in a slightly sarcastic tone, "Do you think that Cave Baba will be found waiting for you? There is always a crowd of thousands, and you are not a wife or mother of a Minister or a Member of Parliament or an MLA or a high-ranked officer who can meet Baba Ji as soon as you reach there. You will go there with enthusiasm but will come back after getting hurt by the crowd."

Mrs. Dixit had expressions of desperation on her face, but suddenly she exhibited a Dunkirk spirit and said, "Come what may, I will take Bhaskar to Baba Ji. He knows everything and will sense our situation. He will call us for sure. Until I meet Baba Ji, I will not come back, whether it takes weeks or months."

Bhaskar's father took his spectacles off. His face was apparently expressing the feelings of reluctant surrender to his wife's decision.

Bhaskar realised that no one could convince his mother to quit the idea of visiting Cave Baba now. He stood up and suddenly felt the shell of the nut lying in his pocket, so he took out that shell and threw it in the courtyard.

As soon as his mother saw that nut, she said, "Why are you keeping this piece of ritha in your pocket?"

Bhaskar said, "So this is ritha? Soapberry? I wanted to ask you what this shell is." Bhaskar left for his room while his parents pondered over his quizzical behaviour.

The Revelation

Bhaskar and his parents were about to reach Cave Baba's ashram when they saw barricades in the middle of the road. Two police constables indicated the vehicle to turn right. Mr. Dixit looked at the driver and said, "Maybe there has been an accident."

The driver laughed and said, "No sir, it seems that you have come here for the first time. Beyond this point, vehicles are not permitted, and one has to go further on foot."

Mr. Dixit looked outside and realised that several hectares of fields had been converted into a parking area. Hundreds of vehicles were parked on the ground. The family left the car in the parking area and walked towards the ashram.

All along the way there were shops on both sides, selling items related to worship, religious books, sweets and there were some small restaurants too. Almost all the residential houses had boards of "ROOMS AVAILABLE" displayed on the walls. Overall, this small village, located in the remote area of the Central Indian region of Bundelkhand, was rejuvenated and transformed into a commercial zone.

A gentleman walking along with them told them that the rent for houses and shops built in this village was at par with that of the prime locations in metro cities, and the land prices were so exorbitant that only Tatas, Birlas or Ambanis could think of buying a piece of land there.

After walking for a mile, the family reached the main gate of the ashram, which was not crowded at all. Mr. Dixit felt some peace of mind by realising that the decision to come today had proved fortuitously correct as the number of people visiting was less today, and so it would be easier for them to have Baba's darshan. The main gate of the ashram was closed but a small side door was open on which security guards wearing dark, grey-colored uniforms were deployed.

Mr. Dixit had just attempted to enter through the gate to go inside when the guard stopped him and said, "Show the pass."

Mr. Dixit got a little shocked and said, "Pass, what kind of pass?"

The guard laughed and said, "Uncle, have you come here for the first time? First go to the Visitors' Wing and get the registration done, then go to the Administrative Wing and get the pass issued. Then you come here. Only after getting a pass issued, you will be allowed to enter inside."

Mr. Dixit's heart sank and with a heavy heart he asked the guard, "Where is the Visitors Wing?"

The guard said, a little irritated, "Are you illiterate? Area maps are displayed prominently at many places. Have a look at one of them, you will know everything. Now, move away and don't block the way."

Bhaskar was listening to the conversation. He got annoyed at the guard's rudeness and wanted to rebuke the guard, but Mr. Dixit dragged him away holding his hand. They headed towards the visitors wing and found a long queue there. They, too, got queued at the end and after two hours, Bhaskar got his family registered. Then, they moved to the administrative wing, which was comparatively less crowded, and the queue was also short. They got the passes within half an hour.

Finally, the Dixit family entered the ashram. They all had to pass through a metal detector just after crossing the gate. Then they reached a wide cemented path with mehndi hedges and beautiful lamp posts on both the sides, along the passage.

Looking at the grandeur of the Ashram, Bhaskar said, "I expected Baba Ji to be living in a cave and presumed that we would reach there by passing through the slippery wet rocks, twigs crunching underfoot and experiencing the smell of animal droppings and stagnant water. But coming here, it feels like we have reached either a five-star hotel or the head office of a multinational company."

Hearing this, Mrs. Dixit frowned at Bhaskar as a signal to keep quiet. Only then, Mr. Dixit said, "Now all Babas are billionaires, they travel by aeroplane, they have fleets of elite-class cars, they wear Ray Ban glasses and use accessories from brands like Mont Blanc and Armani. I think that very soon, all their ashrams will get listed on the stock exchange."

Mrs. Dixit stopped, turned angrily towards him and said, "You too! He is a kid, but you must exercise some restraint." Mr. Dixit got clammed up.

After walking for about a hundred metres, they reached the grand entrance of a palatial building, in front of which a beautiful garden was developed in a circular shape with a big fountain in the centre. They entered the building and reached a well-appointed huge hall in which hundreds of people were already sitting. The volunteers of the ashram were going hither and thither aiding and managing the devotees to get them properly seated. The space was getting filled fast. Bhaskar, along with his parents, got accommodated in a vacant space. After waiting for about one and a half hours, a sweet voice echoed on the loudspeaker that Baba Ji was about to arrive soon, and Baba Ji arrived within a minute.

Baba Ji's age was not above thirty-five. He appeared in a colourful robe with a broad smile on his face. His appearance was attractive and impressive. Baba Ji started his typical mystical process which he was famous for. He picked a devotee randomly from the crowd and called him on the stage. Before he could say anything, he wrote something on a piece of paper and then turned the paper over. Then he asked that devotee to describe the problems he wished to get resolved by Baba Ji to everyone on the public address system. After that, Baba Ji showed and read aloud the paper that he had already written on. Astoundingly, the paper contained the mention of all the problems exactly as shared by the devotee, with suggested solutions.

The whole crowd started cheering for Baba Ji and his miraculous powers. This process went on for about three hours, but Baba Ji did not call any member of the Dixit family. And then, the same melodious voice echoed again on the loudspeaker. It was time for Baba Ji to rest, and the whole hall echoed with the cheers of Baba Ji. Baba Ji got up and left the place.

Bhaskar's mother's hopes were shattered by Baba Ji's departure. She was almost about to cry. People started dispersing and moving out, but Bhaskar and his parents stayed in their place. After some time, only the members of the Dixit family were left in the hall.

Mrs. Dixit was in a shocked state. She could not believe that Baba Ji had not called her. She was crying, feeling that her years of worship and devotion had been in vain. Bhaskar and his father were trying to convince her, but she was not ready to listen to anything.

Observing her, a tall man, who was a volunteer, approached them and tried to find out about the matter. He was speaking loudly and trying to convince her that "Baba Ji felt other people's problems to be more serious than yours and that's why he didn't call you." After a brief discussion with the family, he moved towards the exit and signalled Mr. Dixit to follow him.

Mr. Dixit reached outside and found the person waiting for him. The tall man again signalled to follow him. Mr. Dixit continued to follow him until the tall man stopped behind a tree beside the building. He walked to him.

The tall man said, "Sir, observing your wife's true devotion, I felt a strong urge to help you. I can arrange your personal meeting with Baba Ji. But for this you will have to spend a little."

Mr. Dixit said hesitantly, "How much?"

"Fifty thousand," said the tall man.

Mr. Dixit lost his senses on hearing the amount. With folded hands he said, "Brother, perhaps you have misjudged me. I do not have the capacity to pay that much."

The tall man said, "People are ready to pay up to fifty lakhs to meet Baba Ji and you are refusing to pay a small amount of fifty thousand."

Mr. Dixit said, "I don't know what you think of me. I am a retired school teacher. The amount you have demanded is way beyond my capacity."

The tall man looked troubled. He said, "I don't know why I felt such a strong sympathy for your wife. OK, tell me how much you can pay?"

Mr. Dixit was happy to give a maximum of five hundred rupees, but he did not feel it apt to reduce the demand of the person to the hundredth fraction. Gathering courage, he said, "I can give up to five thousand rupees."

The tall man was dissatisfied by the amount, but he said in a muffled voice, "Okay, give it."

Mr. Dixit gave him the money. The tall man counted the money, took out a slip from his pocket, gave it to Mr. Dixit and said, "Fill in the details quickly."

Mr. Dixit entered the details accordingly. Then he took the slip back and said, "Stay in the hall, I will call you in a while." He left Mr. Dixit behind, walking away briskly.

Everything happened so quickly that Mr. Dixit stood bewildered for a while and then walked towards the hall with a heavy heart. He had only one thought flashing in his mind, that the man had cheated him and usurped his five thousand rupees.

When Mr. Dixit returned to his family, his face lowered. Bhaskar asked him, "Any problem, Papa?"

Mr. Dixit did not answer his question, rather he looked at his wife and said, "I am trying to fix a meeting with Baba Ji."

Mrs. Dixit turned to him and stared as if she did not like his humbug. Bhaskar, looking at his face, said, "What happened, Papa, where did you go?"

Mr. Dixit said in a very low voice, "I sought help from that tall man. He assured me that he would introduce us to Baba Ji."

Bhaskar's face showed a sense of surprise and Mrs. Dixit looked like a glimpse of happiness awakened by hope.

Bhaskar said, "Papa, do you think that a person of his status can introduce us to Baba Ji? I think that he doesn't hold a position that he himself can meet Baba Ji. Anyway, some of Baba Ji's acts seem miraculous. I was also impressed, but a miracle remains a miracle, as long as the method of doing it remains a secret. Once the secret of the trick is revealed, every miracle seems normal. A few years ago, many of the Babas who were in the limelight are in jail now and no one remembers them. People have forgotten them."

Showing false anger towards Bhaskar, Mrs. Dixit gently slapped him on the hand and said, "Shut up, you still have no sense of worldliness. Reading a few books can't bring worldly wisdom."

They waited for more than two hours. It was half past eight in the night. Just then, a few workers came inside the hall carrying mops, brooms and wipers. One of them was carrying a big dustbin and two people were pushing a big machine. Bhaskar sensed that all of them had come to clean the hall and now they'd leave the place. Bhaskar said, "Mother, now let's go from here. Come on, Papa."

Mrs. Dixit got agitated again and said, "I will not even move from here without meeting Baba Ji."

Bhaskar said, "Mother, see the housekeeping staff has arrived to clean the place. Come on now, get up from here. If you want to make a protest over here, then come here again, once the cleaning is done. OK."

Mrs. Dixit held Bhaskar's hand and got up with his support. Bhaskar held on to her as they left the hall. Mr. Dixit was still sad for losing his five thousand rupees, but now he was in a dilemma whether he should tell this to his wife and son.

Bhaskar wanted to go back home as soon as possible. Looking at his father, he said, "The driver of our taxi must be sitting there in the parking lot."

His mother got furious at listening to Bhaskar and stopped. She was not ready to leave under any circumstances.

Mr. Dixit had realised by now that the tall man had swindled him and thus had already given up hope of receiving any response from the rook. So, he decided to forget about it. He focused on his wife and tried to console her by explaining, "If we could not meet Baba Ji today, it does not mean that we will not meet him at all. We will come again after two or three days.

If we remain unsuccessful on that day too, we will come again. It is about nine o'clock in the night; it will take us three hours to reach home. If we leave now, we will reach home at midnight. Now there is no point in staying here today."

Mrs. Dixit made a face as if she had surrendered. They walked towards the main gate of the ashram.

Only then, a volunteer came running to them holding a slip in his hand. He read the names on the slip, Mr. R. S. Dixit, Mrs. Astha Dixit, Mr. Bhaskar Dixit and said, "Are these your names?"

Bhaskar said, "Yes." The employee read the slip again and said, "You people have come from Deri village of Tikamgarh district."

Bhaskar said teasingly, "Yes, this address is also ours, but tell us what happened."

The employee said with great enthusiasm, "Baba Ji wants to meet you."

Hearing this, Mrs. Dixit was extremely surprised and ecstatic. She folded both her hands and said thanks to God and Baba Ji. Mr. Dixit was also very happy, but the best part of his happiness came only from the satisfaction that his hard earned five thousand rupees had not gone in vain. Bhaskar's face exhibited satisfaction rather than happiness. He was happy because his mother was relieved.

The volunteer took them to a lobby room inside the building and gestured to them to sit on a sofa. He pointed to a closed door and told them that Baba Ji would meet them in that room shortly. Meanwhile, a lady attendant brought water and tea for them.

As soon as they finished tea, a man of impressive personality came, greeted them politely and said, "I am the caretaker of the

Ashram and work as a personal assistant to Baba Ji. Baba Ji is waiting for you."

Mrs. Dixit was amazed. She immediately stood up holding her husband's arm with one hand and her son's arm with the other, signalling them to get up and move. Seeing her impatience, the caretaker smiled.

Bhaskar walked inside with his parents and found Baba Ji sitting in front of them on a grand sofa-like chair. He greeted them with folded hands and gestured to sit on the sofa next to them. Despite Baba Ji's gesture towards the sofa, Mrs. Dixit kept moving forward and was about to sit on the carpet near Baba Ji's feet when Baba Ji bent down and stopped her and took her to the sofa himself. Bhaskar and Mr. Dixit sat next to her. Bhaskar was deeply impressed with the politeness of Baba Ji.

Baba Ji said, "Meeting you people is just a coincidence. Why and how, let me tell you in brief. Whenever I stay in the ashram at night, I regularly meet some people in the evening also. The ashram staff scrutinise the details of people and provide them with a 'Privilege Pass'. Those people who I meet here are either from the elite class or the families and close relatives of volunteers. My personal assistant, who is also the caretaker of the ashram, was suspicious of one of the volunteers because of his frequent demand of the 'Privilege Pass'. It was suspected that this volunteer demanded money from the devotees and provided them with the pass by declaring them his relatives. He did the same with you today but got caught red-handed."

Hearing this, both Mrs. Dixit and Bhaskar looked at Mr. Dixit together. Mr. Dixit looked guilty, hesitated a little, but then folded his hands as a gesture of apology.

Baba Ji continued, "My assistant told me that, today again, that employee asked for the 'Privilege Pass' for a family claiming them to be his relatives. As soon as I saw your name and address, I suddenly remembered that my father stayed at this place for a few years and learned astrology and Sanskrit from a great scholar. I do not remember his full name, but his surname was also Dixit. My father used to address him as Acharya Ji, and often talked about his scholastic achievements and unique personality."

Bhaskar had a sense of pride on his face; he said with much enthusiasm, "He was my grandfather."

Baba Ji looked at Bhaskar and said, "I had a similar assumption about your family, and it is a privilege to meet the family of such a divine personality. Whatever education I have received I got from my father only. The education that my father received, he got from Acharya Ji. In this way, Acharya Ji holds a reverend status for me."

Bhaskar felt proud of his grandfather and now his faith in his exceptional achievements turned firmer.

Baba Ji looked at Bhaskar's face and kept gazing for a while and gradually closed his eyes. After a minute, he opened his eyes and smiled mysteriously. Then he shifted his sight to Mrs. Dixit and said, "Mother, you came here with a purpose and now your purpose is a mission for me. I promise you that I will help you with my full abilities. But first you should promise me that you will keep trust in me and my advice."

Mrs. Dixit was puzzled and was unable to presume anything from Baba Ji's assertion. But she got just a little idea that it was her father-in-law whose grace had provided her family an opportunity to receive special treatment at the ashram. Her emotions escaped in the form of tears through his eyes. She folded her hands and said, "We can trust none other than you and it is for this reason that we are here. Your words will be commandments for us. Please, show us the way." Mr. Dixit was also shaking his head, affirming the words of his wife.

Then Baba Ji turned to Mr. Dixit, and said, "I need your commitment too. Sir, would you mind if I ask you some questions?"

The way Baba Ji sought his permission to ask questions, Mr. Dixit simply guessed that the questions would definitely be about some sensitive issue but trying to conceal his thoughts from appearing on his face, Mr. Dixit said, "Yes sir."

Baba Ji smiled and said, "What were your father's expectations of you?"

Mr. Dixit tried to speak but was unable to produce more than a slight stuttering sound. Baba Ji kept smiling while Bhaskar felt a little embarrassed.

Baba Ji continued, "Let me simplify the question. What were Acharya Ji's plans for your career?"

Mr. Dixit replied with extreme bitterness, "He never got time to think about our careers. He never realised the importance of money and always remained insouciant towards the needs of the family."

Baba Ji asked, "Had Acharya Ji ever asked you to learn any of his skills and knowledge?"

Mr. Dixit said, "He always insisted that I learn all his knowledge in Astrology, Astronomy, Vedic Chemistry and other areas of his expertise. But I realised that the knowledge of these obsolete streams couldn't help me to lead a happy life. Then, he finally asked me to attain knowledge of Ayurveda to enable myself to earn a living." Mr. Dixit took deep breaths.

Baba Ji asked him, "Did you follow his advice?"

The question fell like a hammer on Mr. Dixit's conscience. He answered in a loud voice, "No, I didn't follow him. Because I didn't want to…"

Baba Ji interrupted and didn't allow Mr. Dixit to complete, and said to Mr. Dixit, "I am not interested in knowing the reasons. Just tell me whether he compelled you to follow his advice."

Mr. Dixit said, "No, once I got a job, he stopped insisting."

Baba Ji instantly asked, "Was your decision, right?"

Mr. Dixit replied, "Yes, I made the right decision. Had I followed his profession and way of life, I wouldn't have done anything in my life. Now, one can claim my decisions to be wrong. It is common to respect idealistic principles and talk about virtues like altruism, sacrifice, devotion, simplicity and social change, but following them is quite a different thing. Everyone wishes for the rebirth of revolutionaries, but in the neighbourhood only and not in one's own house."

Baba Ji said, "Mr. Dixit, No one can blame you, as every act is governed by the will of God. No one can deviate from the will of God. No one has the right to call your decision wrong because every activity that occurs in this world is done by the will of God. However, God, too, does not impose his will on anyone, but gives them the right to choose. It depends on one's own discretion. Choosing the right option is what we call luck or divine grace. The Right choice is necessary for the attainment of destiny and for that one must have faith in God. Nature signals you when you start deviating from the path of your destiny but recognizing and following those signs depends on one's faith in God. Moreover, understanding the language of signs only is not enough; rather, changing the path according to those signs is more important. Sometimes, there are moments when one turns insecure about the consequences of changing the path, and this is the most crucial moment that decides if you are moving away from destiny or towards it. In fact, people do not get afraid of the situation, they rather, fear assumptions about the consequences. On the other hand, a person who has no doubt in his mind regarding the compliance of divine indications attains his destiny."

Baba Ji continued, "Now the question arises: why is doubt born? Doubt comes only when you start evaluating your destiny in terms of the trivial instances of your life. Life is not an account of profit and loss, but a statement of your credit account in which an increase in faith in God results in an increase in your credit score."

When he finished, Baba Ji kept silent. Mrs. Dixit started feeling a little awkward, so she said, "Baba Ji, please listen to the problem that brought us here. We are worried about our son, Bhaskar…"

Baba Ji interrupted her, "Mother, that is what I am talking about. You think that some evil spirit has haunted your son while your husband wants him to consult a psychiatrist. And with great regards to both of you, none of you is correct. Your son neither needs a psychiatrist, nor an exorcist. He himself will be required to act and your support will be his greatest strength. Give him some time, some freedom. He is your son and will remain forever. I insist you give him fifteen days. Only fifteen days; and for this period, free him from all your expectations. Let him go wherever he wants, let him do what he wants. And, mother, don't get worried, for these fifteen days, his safety and well-being will be my responsibility."

Bhaskar said, "Baba Ji, may I ask you something?"

Baba Ji smiled. "Sure. However, I know what is going on in your mind, but it will be more appropriate to listen to it in your words."

Bhaskar said, "Are dreams worth following?"

Baba Ji replied, "Our Vedic tradition of knowledge considers dreams as the most reliable sources of insight. Dreams indicate one's capability to interact with the supreme consciousness and show you glimpses of reality in this illusory world. However, many people think the other way and consider dreams to be illusions and the world to be real. Dreams make you realise the distinction between soul and body; and show you the path to realise the illusory nature of the body and the world around us."

Bhaskar asked him, "Is it possible that a person who died sixteen years ago can send a message today? Is it scientifically reasonable?"

Baba Ji smiled and said, "The problem lies in the absurdity of considering scientific evidence only to be proof of truth. Science cannot transcend senses and language cannot express silence. These are linear concepts, while the Universe is multidimensional and multi fold. So, there are many things which are way beyond the reach of science. Consciousness has four stages. The first three—waking, dreaming and deep sleep—are states which exist with duality of senses and mind. The fourth state is Turiya, in which consciousness is neither inward, nor outward, nor both inward and outward. This state is beyond the senses, knowledge and reason. It cannot be described, comprehended or thought. This is pure consciousness that is nondual; this is one without a second. A person who experiences this state of consciousness attains unification with universal consciousness or the infinite spirit. Thus, he attains a state that is ever-existing, ever-conscious and all-pervasive. This is a state that permeates the other three states. It is no surprise for an exceptional personality like him. Acharya Ji has reached pure awareness of his own self, which is nondual. He has become one with everyone and everything. For him, the known, the knower and the knowledge have unified and become one."

Bhaskar said, "It seems very confusing to me. I cannot understand clearly. So, are all dreams worth catching? Is my dream only an apparition or is it a kind of encoded message? Baba Ji, please guide me."

Baba Ji smiled again. "I would like to give you an analogy. Consider Dreams as a television channel. You can watch the programs only if you keep the antenna in correct alignment and calibration. The more powerful the antenna, the clearer the visuals will be. The lack of clarity in the output indicates misalignment of the antenna. A channel telecasts programs round the clock, but you watch the programs related to your interests only. Similarly, one's dreams are related to one's emotions, fancy, fear, imagination, intellect and knowledge. All these are variables only and they may only affect the efficiency and reception quality of an antenna. But they can't affect the content of the program being telecast."

Baba Ji stopped for a while, and then said in a grave voice, "Bhaskar, as far as I can analyse, your grandfather has left a message for you, and you need to find it by yourself. You have reached a square, where you must take the path of your choice. If you commit a mistake in choosing the right one, you will never reach the goal that is provisioned for you. So, it's your take, follow your heart. Put your reason aside, for a while. Listen to your fancy, listen to your instinct, listen to your inner self, let your fears and doubts come to the surface. Then seek the answers to the questions that trouble you. Once you find the answers, the troubles will go away and you will get a genuine reason to follow your destiny, with full commitment and without any worries or dilemmas. May God bless you."

Baba Ji then stood up and greeted them with folded hands. Everyone stood with him. Baba Ji turned back and went inside. Bhaskar's mother was still in a state of enchanting awe, and thus she remained standing like a statue. Bhaskar shook her hand to bring her back to normalcy and gestured to ask her to leave the place. Bhaskar held her hand, and then they turned and moved towards the exit.

In the meantime, the caretaker rushed to them and handed over an envelope to Mr. Dixit, and said, "Sir, your amount of five thousand rupees. The volunteer returned it. Please keep it." Mr. Dixit received the envelope and moved along with his family, towards the exit.

The Reconnaissance

Bhaskar was in his grandfather's room. This time, he had the key to the tiny brass lock. He opened the almirah, which had three shelves in it. The top shelf contained only a small chrome finished bottle of about half a litre capacity, shining brightly. He tried to lift it, but it seemed to him very heavy, contrary to his appraisal. He was a little surprised. Then, he lifted it carefully with both hands and guessed that it weighed about seven to eight kilograms. The bottle had a handwritten label on it.

He blew the dust away and read the label: "Pure Mercury, Net Weight Seven Ser." Now, he understood the secret of its extraordinary weight. That was a half litre glass bottle, containing about six and a half kilograms of mercury. He remembered his school days when he learned that the density of mercury is more than thirteen times that of normal water. He also knew that Ser was a unit of weight used earlier in India that equals around 933 grams.

He put the bottle back on the shelf and focused on the middle shelf containing a leather bag, while the lower shelf was empty. He lifted the bag and found that it contained three separate pockets. He opened the first pocket and found a packet weighing nearly a hundred grams. The packet was wrapped in leather and tied with a leather string. He placed the packet on the bench. He opened the other pocket and found another packet that seemed exactly similar to the first packet but was slightly heavier than that. Then, he opened the third pocket, which contained a rolled piece of red cloth tied with a leather string.

Bhaskar couldn't understand anything, but the packaging indicated that those were some very important things. Bhaskar opened the cloth roll first. The roll contained another white cloth. Bhaskar opened the cloth, which was basically a document containing a conversion table of traditional Indian Units to SI units. However, it was not exhaustive; it contained only the conversion of Ser, Tola, Masha and Ratti units into grams and kilograms. Bhaskar couldn't understand why such trivial information was kept so securely.

Then he opened the first packet, untied the string and opened the leather sheet. He found a leather pouch inside. The pouch was neatly sewed and labelled with a paper slip indicating "White Powder Net Weight 6.5 Tola (78 Masha) 1 Ratti per Tola."[3] He gently squeezed and patted the pouch and small traces of a white powder fell from it.

He didn't know what to make of it, so he unpacked another packet. The other packet too, contained a similar leather pouch, labelled as "Yellow powder Net weight 7.5 Tola (90 Masha) $1_{1/4}$ Ratti per Tola." He comprehended easily that the labels indicated the weight of the corresponding powder in the packet, but the measurements given in "Ratti per Tola" were beyond his understanding. He thought that these must be proportions in order to prepare some compound or mixture, but other than that he was clueless. After a while of observing the contents, he packed everything in the same way it was packed before and locked the almirah.

He sat on the wooden bench and tried to put together some meaning or purpose of the objects in order to get a clue. He kept on brooding and speculating for more than an hour, but nothing clicked. Bhaskar was extremely disappointed and

---

[3] **Ratti/Masha/Tola:** *traditional Indian units of measurement of mass, esp. used for weighing precious metals and powdered medicines. 1 Ratti equals 0.1134 grams, 1 Masha equals 8 Ratti, and 1 Tola equals 12 Masha.*

dejected when he remembered Cave Baba's assertion, *"Your Dada Ji had left a message for you."* So, he started thinking about the message and suddenly he remembered a postal slip he had come across in the room. He recalled that the slip was in a bundle in the loft.

As soon as he recollected this, he moved lightning fast, brought a stool from another room and got the bundle down from the loft. He opened the bundle and took the slip out of the bag. He observed the slip minutely. It was clear that the slip was an acknowledgement of a registered post or parcel, but the date was not traceable. Perhaps the stamp was affixed in haste, leaving only a partial imprint, and the ink had also faded badly with the passage of time.

After the continuous efforts of half an hour, Bhaskar shouted, "Yes!" He was successful in tracing the name of the post office branch as "Head Post Office Panna." He ran out of the room shouting, "Papa! Papa!"

Mr. Dixit was sitting in a chair in the courtyard. He heard Bhaskar calling him, so he replied, "I am here."

Bhaskar reached there and said, "Papa, I found an acknowledgement slip that had a stamp of Head Post Office Panna, a bottle of mercury and two powders. Had he ever been to Panna? Did he have a close friend in Panna?"

Mr. Dixit replied, "I have no idea. You may be wondering that I do not have information related to my father. You are already aware that there was friction in our relationship. In my opinion, your Dada Ji was doing something expected only from opulent families. If one has abundant wealth and resources for self and family, then one may continue a knowledge-seeking adventure without any desire for financial returns. I was not happy with him, and neither were my brothers. I felt that he was doing injustice to his family by not using his knowledge and skills commercially. Had he wished, he could have provided us with the most advanced amenities and facilities. Either he didn't have the capability to use his talent commercially or he didn't care about us. That's why I refrained from him and his intellectual affairs. We lived in the same house, but I was completely unconcerned about his activities. What was he doing? To whom was he teaching? Where did he go? Who came to meet him? I never tried to find out anything. The only concern I used to have about him was whether he received all the meals on time. And later, your mother's arrival in the family made me free from this concern too. But don't worry; I have a resource for getting the information."

Mr. Dixit also told him that mercury, being an important ingredient in Ayurvedic medicines, is the most common substance to be kept by Ayurvedic practitioners, so there was nothing significant about it and the powders must be some medicine.

Then, Mr. Dixit told him about a priest of a temple located on the outskirts of the village. He said, "The priest was once an aide to your grandfather. Along with helping him with his daily chores, he learned a little bit of astrology and chanting of some basic Sanskrit Shlokas used for routine worship methods and rituals. He may prove to be useful as he remained in close contact with your Dada Ji for many years. He may possess vital information."

Bhaskar asked his father, "Is he trustworthy enough, so can we tell him the actual purpose of seeking information?"

Mr. Dixit replied, "It is not a matter of being trustworthy. The area we live in is very backward. If the matter comes out, people will start gossiping. There is no need to reveal your specific purpose. Just get to the track gradually without revealing your real motive. Let him realise that everything he is narrating is interesting. Then, he will tell you everything he remembers. After that, it will be your job to sift through all the information to find useful facts."

He continued, "Today, while coming back home from my evening walk, I will visit the temple and invite him to have a cup of tea with me tomorrow. He will come for sure. So, once he reaches here and gets settled, you may join the discussion. You should remember that enquiry & discussion are two different disciplines. The purpose and operation of both are totally different. It depends on your cleverness that the person sitting before you may not realise that he is being enquired. Let him keep talking and you keep making enquiries. Let him feel that he spoke only what he himself wanted to share and you get the job done."

The Probe

Bhaskar walked out of the room and heard the sound of conversation from the drawing room. He headed to the drawing room and saw that a person dressed like a saint was sitting with his father. The man was wearing a tilak made with two vertical lines, similar to the 'U' mark, made with yellow sandalwood paste. There was also a red vertical line in the middle of the mark. His throat and arms also carried yellow marks made with sandalwood paste.

Bhaskar greeted him by folding both his hands and bowing his head. In response to the greetings, he blessed the boy by lifting his hands.

He looked at Bhaskar's father and said, "This is your son, isn't he? I saw him when he was a kid but have heard a lot about his exceptional intelligence. This is the law of Nature. The prodigious talent of Acharya Ji had to pass on to his progeny."

Then he looked at Bhaskar and said, "Son, do you remember anything about your grandfather or not? As far as I can remember, you were around six or seven years old at the time of Acharya Ji's departure."

Bhaskar said, "I was eight. I remember a few things. He used to write a new shloka everyday in my notebook and I used to learn it the same day. I have only a few fixed frames of him in my memory: Him, reading a book in his recliner, writing something on his writing desk, sitting against the attic wall on the terrace in winter and grinding something with a mortar and pestle, squatting on his teakwood bench."

The priest said with great enthusiasm, "You do not remember me, but I can clearly recall your childhood days with your grandfather."

Bhaskar asked, "What did Dada Ji think about me?"

The priest replied with great affinity, "You were the apple of his eye. He considered you to be the only—" The priest stopped abruptly and suddenly started to cough.

Bhaskar got up and handed a glass of water to the priest. The priest looked at him and at Mr. Dixit. Then he drank the water and put the glass back on the table. In the meanwhile, Bhaskar felt as if his father was frowning at the priest and grinding his teeth at him. However, he rejected the thought by considering it only a deceptive vision because his father appeared happy and was smiling.

Bhaskar asked him, "Have you been a student of Dada Ji?"

The priest replied, "I got the privilege of serving him, and during that time, I learned many things from him."

The priest seemed to be getting emotional. He further said, "I hailed from a nearby village. I was seven years old when my parents passed away. The financial condition of the family was very bad. Feeling pity, a shopkeeper from the village gave me a job in his shop. I used to work at his shop from early morning to late night and, in return, got two meals a day, and old clothes to wear. I worked there for about ten years. Once, Acharya Ji came for the treatment of the shopkeeper's son and stayed there for a day. The shopkeeper deployed me to his service during his stay. I was already aware of Acharya Ji's name and fame. I told him that I am a Brahmin by birth. I have not received formal education but can read and write. I just want to learn basic religious work and worship rituals, so that I can earn my living by working according to my social status. Acharya Ji assured me that he'd give me education, free food and accommodation. I had found God in the form of Acharya

Ji. After fifteen days, I left the job and went to his shelter. I stayed with him for about six years, helped him with his daily chores. I used to clean his room, take care of his horse by leaving it in the meadow near the pond in the morning and bringing it to the stable in the evening. I used to massage Acharya Ji's feet at night just before sleeping. In the rest of the free time, he used to teach me."

Bhaskar asked, "So you stayed in his company for six years?"

The priest said, "Yes, I stayed in his service. He was such a pleasant and gracious personality that staying in his company was a divine experience. He used to live with such a simplicity that no one could guess his exceptional qualities by his appearance. He could foresee things. Let me tell you one incident. He used to listen to the news on the radio in the evening and many others also used to gather, every day at that time, on a platform built at the front of your house. Once, it was told that the then Prime Minister Shri Lal Bahadur Shastri had agreed to visit Tashkent for bilateral talks with Pakistan. Acharya Ji seemed sad at the news. When asked about his melancholy, he told us that the visit to Tashkent may prove to be fatal for the Prime Minister. After two days, we got the news of the demise of the prime minister in Tashkent. Acharya Ji had a supernatural ability to read the past, comprehend the present and sense the future. Despite all these qualities, he was a down-to-earth person. He helped me to get appointed as the priest of the temple. Then, I shifted myself from this house to a room located on the temple premises. After that, I seldom met him."

Bhaskar said, "Were there other students also who were being taught by Dada Ji?"

The priest said, "Many; Acharya Ji never accepted more than three students at a time. When I was with him, there were two students for about a year, then another one joined and then one left. Similar things always used to happen. Acharya Ji's disciples were from distant places. I remember a few names of places, like Puri, Odisha, Vidarbha area, Uttarkashi, Jammu, Bengal etc."

Bhaskar said, "So Dada Ji used to teach the students from distant places only and not from our area and state."

The priest replied, "No, it was not so. I hailed from a nearby village. He educated a student from Tikamgarh and later educated his son too. And yes, one of his all-time favorite students was from Panna."

Bhaskar wished to shout and jump with joy as he finally reached his point of interest. So, he continued the discussion cleverly to extract the desired information. The priest told him about one Vishnu Kant Shastri who was the favourite student of his grandfather.

The priest said, "Shastri Ji stayed here prior to the period of my service, but he used to come to meet Acharya Ji at least once a year. He was a brilliant student. I met him twice. He was a very humble person. He invited me to visit the temples of Panna too and gave his address."

Bhaskar said, "I have a desire to visit the temples of Panna. May you share his address with me? It will be very useful to have a local reference."

The priest replied happily, "Definitely, yes."

Bhaskar gave him a notepad and a pen. The priest wrote the address and then departed.

Exploring the Lost Ends

Bhaskar reached the town famous for its temples and for being the only district in the country blessed with diamond fields. He reached the area as told by the priest. He came to know that the area was a dense locality spread around four square miles, accommodating nearly a thousand families. He reached a pan shop in the square. The small shop was labelled as a pan shop but there were many chocolates and candy boxes on the counter. Strings of wafers and potato chips packets of various brands were hung on both sides of the opening. The shopkeeper was a middle-aged person.

Bhaskar said to him, "Hello uncle, I have come here after a long time. Earlier, I came with my father when I was a kid, about twelve years ago. A person named Shastri Ji used to live here in this area. He was a great scholar of Sanskrit and a fine astrologer. I don't remember the exact location of his house. Can you help me find his house?"

The shopkeeper made a gesture to stop him from speaking and then said, "Yes, yes, I got it. I will guide you to his house, but if you have come here to meet Shastri Ji, then it will serve no purpose to go there. Shastri Ji was a great scholar, and he enjoyed a great reputation. Apart from general public, many political leaders and high-ranking officials were his devotees. However, he never differentiated among people because of social status. He treated the elite and ordinary people in a similar way. Around three years ago, he suddenly stopped meeting people. It was thought that it may be due to some health issue. But there was no such matter. Even at the age of seventy, he was physically fit and remained fully active. To everyone's surprise, one day he left his house. All his family members, his followers and people of the locality tried to stop him. They kept arguing, requesting and persuading, but he didn't stop. There were many conceptions in the air. Few people thought that his family members had started earning money by misusing his name and, due to this, he went to some unknown place, and few said that his renunciation was predestined and many more. He went and then never came back. Now, only his memories are left. Some people say that he has gone to the Himalayas. Some people say that he was seen once or twice in the dense forest near Ajaygarh. God only knows where he is now."

Bhaskar felt his heart sinking, as if everything was finished. The speculative trail that he followed to decode his dream ended in a blind alley. He thought it to be useless to proceed further. But he made up his mind to visit Shastri Ji's house and he moved to his destination after acquiring information about the exact location of the house from the shopkeeper.

Bhaskar reached a big house, prominently marked as "Shastri House." He parked his motorcycle and rang the doorbell. After a moment, a man aged around sixty years appeared at the door. Bhaskar greeted him, but without responding he asked roughly, "What's the matter?"

Bhaskar said, "Uncle, my name is Bhaskar, and I came here to meet Vishnu Shastri Ji."

The man looked irritated and replied a little rudely, "Whosoever you are, Shastri Ji has gone. Do not ask where, because even we don't know." The man turned back without any concern for Bhaskar's reaction.

Bhaskar wondered if he could settle this unexpected situation with his knack of creating stories. He evaluated the situation and planned to create a fictional setting accordingly. He spoke a little loudly. "Uncle, I have to meet the legal heir of Mr. Vishnu Shastri. Please send either his wife or his son or his daughter."

The man appeared again instantly, and with a crooked smile, said, "Please tell me, I am his son." He asked Bhaskar to come inside and offered him to sit on one of the chairs placed in the veranda and expressed his apologies absurdly, and said, "Many people used to visit daily without a purpose, so I got a little irritated. Please forget it."

Bhaskar came instantly to the point and said, "Uncle, my name is Bhaskar Dixit and I have come from Deri, a village in Tikamgarh District."

The man said, "Are you from Acharya Ji's family?"

Bhaskar replied, "Yes, Acharya Ji was my grandfather. A few days ago, a bank official approached my father and told him that they had found an account, held jointly by my grandfather and Shastri Ji. These two old men opened a term deposit for an amount of one thousand rupees and then forgot about it. The deposit was renewed for around forty years and now the amount has grown a hundred times. My father submitted the death certificate of my grandfather to the bank, but the bank officials say that it can be paid only to Shastri Ji as he is alive. So, I need the signature of Shastri Ji on the claim documents. Once the claim gets paid, we will distribute the amount equally between us. My father wished to come here, but due to some health problems he couldn't come and so he sent me."

The man smiled absurdly, "No problem, give me the papers, I will give you, his signature."

Bhaskar felt a bit nervous about his demand for documents, but he exhibited full confidence and said, "Sure, please call Shastri Ji. Actually, my meeting with him is more important than his signature."

The man turned a bit annoyed and said, "Kid, you seem well educated, but you haven't gained worldly wisdom till now. I have been operating my father's account even in his absence for three years. I have been working as a clerk for the last thirty years in the local municipal office and just five years are left for my superannuation. I have expertise in such matters. You cannot imagine the kind of feats I have accomplished. This is just a small bank matter; I have made the dead people do a sale deed of property. Don't worry, give me the documents."

Bhaskar felt stuck in a tight corner. Suddenly, he smiled and said, "Uncle, these bank officials are smart enough to smell all such things. They require the person to turn up at any nearby branch of the bank and only after that, will the claim be processed."

The man looked dejected, and after shaking his head a few times, he said, "These people of the old generation are not practical, they prefer morality and ethics, even to their life. They have many problems with the current social values and thus cannot tolerate our happiness. If there is an opportunity to earn some money, then what's wrong with availing it? My father became extremely angry when he came to know that my younger brother had accepted some money from a few of his followers. So, first he stopped meeting with visitors and one day decided to forsake family life."

Bhaskar put expressions of sympathy on his face and said, "I can understand your disappointment. Do you not have any information about his current location?"

The man said, "He, confidentially, gave me the address by saying that he should be contacted only in the event of the death of his wife— my mother, because he owes his wife some rituals to be completed. He also gave me a strict warning to keep his address secret. However, that's not a problem as an amount of fifty thousand rupees is worth taking the risk of getting chided by him. You can understand his ruthlessness. I will tell you his address, but how can I trust your commitment to share the amount with me."

Bhaskar replied, "Sir, it is a matter of my trust in you, because the payment will be made through an account payee cheque in the name of Shastri Ji. So, you need to take care of me."

The man told Bhaskar about the location.

Bhaskar said, "Uncle, keep assured, come what may, I owe you fifty thousand rupees."

Facing the Ferals

Bhaskar's bike was moving slowly on a narrow path with long grass on both the sides. As soon as he took a sharp turn on the meandering trail, he saw a humongous tree lying across the track. It was a Peepal tree which must have been around thirty metres high, and its trunk had a diameter of about three metres.

He stopped his bike there and inspected the tree. He realised that his luxury of taking a bike ride was over and an eventual hiking venture was about to commence as there was no other option available to move further. He parked the bike on the main stand and locked its handle.

When he looked at the bike, he remembered that his father had always taken great care of it. The bike was about six years old but appeared pristine as there was not a single scratch on it. Once, Bhaskar's uncle had taken his bike and returned with a broken turn indicator lamp. Then Father scolded him badly for his carelessness and got the bike repaired immediately. Bhaskar did not find it appropriate to leave his father's bike at such a place and go ahead, but he didn't have any other option. He unlocked the handle of the bike and pushed it for a short distance from the trail and laid it down in the middle of the grass and then locked the handle.

He went back to the trail and looked in the direction of the bike. It was not visible from there, so after turning convinced, he climbed on the trunk of the tree lying on the way and jumped to the other side. He walked fast. After walking for half an hour, he reached an open rocky ground in the middle of the forest with no trees. The total area of the ground was not more than a hectare. There were only tiny grassy weeds growing between the rocks.

He felt a little relieved. He reached at the centre of the ground and decided to take a rest. He sat on a stone slightly raised above the ground. Only then he heard a rustling noise, followed by a loud gasp and a choked scream. Panicked, he stood up quickly and looked all around while making a complete rotation but didn't notice any movement. Various thoughts started clicking in his mind. He now remembered that he was in Panna National Park, which was a tiger reserve.

Suddenly, he saw a leopard climbing a tree holding a rabbit in its mouth at the far end of the open area. Bhaskar stood like a statue; even his eyelids were not blinking. He made up his mind to run but realised that no matter how fast he ran, he could not run faster than a leopard. He kept his eyes fixed on the same tree on which he had seen the leopard climbing. Now he could neither see the leopard nor any of its activities.

He tried recalling all the things he had read about leopards. He knew that a leopard could run at a speed of about fifty-five kilometers per hour, but at this speed it cannot go more than two hundred metres. His mathematical aptitude got to work, and he calculated that the leopard was about a hundred metres away. If the leopard attacked him, he had to run more than hundred metres in the opposite direction. Then he realised that the leopard had just hunted, so it would take about three to four hours for him to regain its energy level.

This realisation brought him some relief. Gathering full courage, he started walking in the opposite direction of the location where he had spotted the leopard. In his heart, he was only praying to God, "May I be heading in the right direction." He kept walking among the trees. Now he didn't have any idea of direction or his location. He was just walking at a fast pace.

Suddenly, he recalled what his mother often quoted as his grandfather's catchphrase. *"When things seem out of your control, leave everything to God, without any doubt and without thinking about the consequences."*

Bhaskar followed the dictum and he had followed it for the first time in his life. His mother had also narrated to him the interpretation given by his grandfather that *"Under normal circumstances, we are unable to do this because we want to get the outcome of a situation according to our expectations and are not ready to accept the possibility of an outcome contrary to our wishes. Despite knowing everything, we are afraid lest God's decision will turn out to be contrary to our expectations. That's why we keep calculating profit and loss, thinking, why drag God into trivial matters? I'll deal with it myself."*

Now Bhaskar was neither thinking nor planning anything, he was just walking. He had left everything to God. Then he saw a trail in front of him; he regained some hope and started running. Very soon he stopped because there was a big tree lying across the track. Perhaps it was the same tree where he had left his bike. His heart sank at once. He jumped across the tree and started looking for his bike. He found his bike in the status quo he left. He felt extremely disappointed.

He lifted his eyes to the sky. He could see the sky only in the form of random blue spots due to the dense trees. He whispered, "God, I asked you to show me the right path and you sent me back to the starting point. I didn't like this joke."

He straightened up his bike, put the key in the ignition and took the riding position. He wore his helmet, and as soon as he straightened the kick lever to start the engine, he heard a growling sound. He turned to his left and the sight made him tremble and brought a heart quake. A huge white tiger was standing in the middle of the trail. Its chatoyant eyes were glowing like coals, mouth slightly open exhibiting razor-sharp incisors. It was making a low growling sound. Bhaskar felt as if he was paralysed. He was completely thoughtless and was unable even to move his fingers. Suddenly, there was a deafening sound.

The Redeemer

Bhaskar opened his eyes and saw a thatched roof. He got up in a huff and then sat down. He looked around and realised that he was in a hut made of bamboo and grass. An earthen lamp and a canister were kept in one corner of the room and a small mat was kept in the other corner. In the third corner he himself was lying on a mat and in the fourth corner there was a door.

He didn't remember anything about how he got there. What he remembered was a huge white tiger standing in the middle of the trail. It gradually moved towards him, and, in the meanwhile, he heard a loud sound. Then, there was complete darkness before his eyes and after that he woke up in this hut. When he tried to check the time, he found that his wristwatch was missing. He stood up, pulled the door slowly and opened it. When he came out with his head bowed, the sun was shining. He realised that the hut was built on a mound. He walked around the hut and saw his bike parked below the mound. His helmet was lying nearby. When he reached there, he saw that his watch and key were kept inside the helmet. One side of the bike had dents and scratches.

Then he heard a voice from behind. "So, you have come to your senses." Bhaskar turned around and saw a man like a sage standing there. His hair, beard and moustache were completely white, and he wore a tilak made with two vertical lines, similar to the "U" mark, made with yellow sandalwood paste and one red vertical line in the middle of the mark, made with red colour. He had only a white towel wrapped around his waist and was wearing wooden clogs. Apart from this, there was no other accessory on his body.

Bhaskar folded his hands and said, "Sir, who are you and where am I?"

The sage smiled and said, "I am also a human being like you, and you are with me."

Bhaskar got a little irritated by his answer. He said, "Sir, I meant that what is your name, where do you live, what are you doing here and what is the name of this place?"

The sage smiled again and said, "I couldn't understand till now why everyone has a deep fascination with names. May the nature of a person or the climate of a place change with name? If the nomenclature of a deer and a lion is interchanged, will their nature also change? Will the deer turn into a predator, or will the lion start eating grass? Since this cannot happen, the value of a name is zero."

Bhaskar's curiosity currently was to get the desired answers to his questions. Bhaskar kept his hands folded and said, "Sir, I just want to know how I reached here. Who are you? What are you doing in the wild?"

The sage again smiled and said, "Son, I am doing the same thing in this forest that you have come to do. The only difference is that I came here voluntarily, and you are brought by the circumstances."

The sage pointed to the front with his finger and said, "I only brought you here from that clump."

Bhaskar understood that the sage was in no mood to give a straight answer. He got down on his knees with folded hands and said, "Sir, my name is Bhaskar Dixit, and I am a resident of a village in Tikamgarh district, about a hundred kilometres from here. I came here to meet a famous scholar, Shastri Ji of Panna."

The sage suddenly narrowed his eyes, and then closed them. After some time, he opened his eyes and then a big smile appeared on his face. He said, "Are you the grandson of Acharya Ji? It was great to see you. Tell me why you wanted to meet me?"

Bhaskar's face had mixed expressions of joy and excitement; he went ahead and touched the feet of the sage. Bhaskar said, "What a wonderful coincidence, even though I could not find you, you found me."

The sage said, "This is all our illusion, we think that we have done it, while we have done nothing. Everything that happens is already fixed and well-defined. If it has to happen, it will happen. Man starts considering himself as the creator and then his actions start going against nature. By the way, seeing you today, my faith in destiny has become firmer. Tell me what you want to know."

Bhaskar said, "Sir, can you tell me about my grandfather?"

The sage said, "You want to know something about Acharya Ji that you do not know. The aspects you didn't get information about from your father or anyone else. Am I right?"

Bhaskar said, "Yes sir."

The sage smiled and asked, "Just a curiosity to know about your grandfather couldn't have led you to seek me in this wild. Come to the point?"

Bhaskar narrated the dream sequence in detail and shared the conclusion derived by Cave Baba. Bhaskar kept silent for a while and then said, "I realise that it is not an ordinary dream. The impulse of the dream is so strong that it is unforgettable. As per the conclusion derived by Cave Baba, I looked for any hint left by my grandfather. I searched Dada Ji's room and found a postal slip issued by Head Post Office Panna. That paved a way for me to approach you."

The Sage said, "You must have heard the stories of Acharya Ji's scholarship, his sharp intelligence and unlimited knowledge. Apart from this, there was another aspect of his personality, more superior than all these, which brought him near divinity in this human world and that was his reluctance to material achievements. But despite all this divinity, he was also a human being. He, too, had a desire to groom his children to be better than himself. His children didn't take any interest in his knowledge and skills. Acharya Ji never wanted to impose his choice on his children. He rather wanted his children to explore new dimensions in the field of knowledge, art, skill, science or literature, and not to treat wealth as a yardstick of life. However, things didn't go as he wished, but that didn't disappoint him. He was never upset with his children. He knew that the realisation of destiny is the true success of life, and the direction of their destiny is different from that of him."

Bhaskar said, "Sir, did you ever meet him after my birth? Did he ever talk about me?"

The sage smiled and said, "You have the spark of Acharya Ji. Your arrival bestowed him with celestial joy. His happiness knew no bounds. During his last two years, he felt a little worried. I don't know what he visualised, but he used to express his anxiety about the changing parameters of society. He told me that in the near future, the definition of prosperity will be based on the availability of money and the financial status of people will decide their esteem in the society. I used to visit him at least once a year. He was very affectionate to me. He trusted me and often assigned me some personal tasks. It was my penultimate visit to him, about eighteen months before his demise. He gave me a letter and a parcel to post because your village didn't have a post office till then. He instructed me to first send the letter, through a registered post with acknowledgement due, and post the parcel only after the acknowledgement slip is received. I did accordingly. Neither did I ask him about the contents of the letter and the parcel, nor did he share it with me."

The sage turned silent, and it seemed he was lost in the past. He took a deep breath and continued, "On my next visit, which was my last visit to him, nearly seven months before his departure to the heavenly abode, I handed over the slip to him. He said to me, *'Vishnu, life is transitory, and the world is illusory, but consciousness is eternal. There is no certainty that you may meet me again, but my consciousness will be there, forever. Once someone matches the level of my consciousness, he may feel me and interact with me. You are one of my fiduciaries who will help my consciousness to get connected with my intellectual heir. He is still very young, and I don't have enough time to wait for him to grow up. It is your responsibility to give him a lesson that Ayurveda or Astrology or Astronomy is not the final pinnacle of knowledge for every individual. There is no particular branch of knowledge in which mastery is essential. The strength and prowess of an elephant, a lion, a monkey and a frog cannot be compared. All of them have one or the other skill which they have mastered. It is wrong to say that an elephant is better than a lion, or vice versa. You cannot compare the greatness of Mahatma Gandhi and Rabindra Nath Tagore. Gold and steel cannot be compared, as both have their own specific uses. It is foolish to make swords of gold and ornaments of steel. I am handing over this responsibility to you so that this should not happen.'*

"I couldn't understand it clearly, so I said, 'Acharya Ji, May God confer eternity on you. Your every word is an order for me. So, if you feel that your grandson will be educated by me, I will come here and stay as long as required.' At my statement, Acharya Ji laughed and said, *'Vishnu, you need not come to him. When his destiny requires, he will find you.'*"

Bhaskar exclaimed with surprise, "Dada Ji knew that I would approach you."

The sage laughed. "He was above any clairvoyance and foreseeing. I didn't even know that you would come. Now, I am sure that he was the designer of your destiny."

Bhaskar was silent. He got goosebumps due to the extreme thrill. At the same time, he was also experiencing a feeling of pride and honour for his grandfather.

Bhaskar asked the sage, "If Dada Ji had a plan for my future, why did he not share it with my father?"

The sage had an ironic smile on his face and said, "A sleeping person can be woken up, but not a person who pretends to be sleeping. There is a temple on the outskirts of your village. Spare some time to go there and meet the priest of that temple."

Bhaskar said, "I know him. I had a long discussion with him just three days ago. He didn't mention any such thing."

The sage said, "I assume your father was with you the whole time. Do you know that Acharya Ji breathed his last in the lap of that priest?"

Bhaskar was stunned. He remained statuesque for some time. He felt as if his head was going to explode. He felt the earth spinning and he gradually sat down on the ground. The sage came near him and patted his head with affection. He said, "Don't worry, son. This time you need to meet him alone. Everything will appear crystal clear to you."

Bhaskar asked the sage, "Sir, what do you think I should do now?"

The sage said, "What I think doesn't make any sense. I can only think that my role in this grand setting is over now. Let me tell you the details of another fiduciary. You may note down his name and address."

Bhaskar said, "Yes sir, let me bring a pen and paper. It is there in my bag." He rushed to his bike. Bhaskar brought the paper and pen, and the sage wrote down the details.

Returning the paper to Bhaskar, the sage said, "Your next destination is Gangotri."

Bhaskar said with a little surprise, "Gangotri, Uttarakhand?" and focused on the paper, going through the details written by the sage.

Bhaskar folded the paper, put it in his pocket and then, very politely asked, "Sir, one question is still straining me. You told me that you brought me from the clump. But how did you find me?"

The sage said, "There is nothing like suspense in it. I was sitting outside my hut when I heard a thunderous vroom with continuous honking and then a rumbling sound. Those were the sounds of your motorbike when you had the accident."

Bhaskar exclaimed with surprise, "Accident! I didn't have any accident. And the Tiger! Did you see the Tiger? A huge white Tiger!"

The sage laughed loudly. "I think you had a dream again. There are no tigers in this part of the forest, and you are talking about a white tiger. There are no white tigers in the whole state." The sage was still laughing intermittently.

Bhaskar said, "Sir, believe me. I was about to start my bike, when I saw a huge white tiger standing across the trail, just near the fallen Peepal tree. Let's go, I will show you."

The sage narrowed his eyebrows and said, "You are talking about the fallen Peepal tree, where there is tall grass on both sides of the trail."

Bhaskar said, "Yes, exactly."

The sage said with surprise, "What! That place is about seven to eight kilometres away from here."

Bhaskar said, puzzled, "How is it possible? I remember everything clearly. I rode about twelve kilometres from the main road and stopped due to the blockage created by that giant tree. I left my bike there. I trekked for about half an hour and reached an open rocky ground. I saw a leopard and rushed from there. I lost my way and after some time, I again reached the same spot of the grounded Peepal tree. I picked up my bike, started it and at the same moment, I saw a huge white tiger standing across the trail and then I remember waking up in your hut."

The sage said, "It is correct that the location of the fallen tree is about twelve kilometres from the highway, but the spot is around eight kilometres away from here as the highway is just four kilometres away from here, and the rocky ground you are talking about is undoubtedly a habitat of leopards and is around three kilometres away from that Peepal tree. So, all your descriptions seem correct, but a tiger and especially a white tiger cannot be believed because there are no tigers in this area of forest, and there are no white tigers in the whole state. You may have gotten confused. Similarly, you are confused about the last spot you remember."

Bhaskar said with full confidence, "Sir, I am not confused, not even a little. I am damn sure."

The sage suddenly reacted as if he remembered something. He lifted his hands up, looked at the sky and said, "O, the Almighty, the omniscient and the omnipresent, you are everywhere. You cannot let the words of your true devotees down."

Then, he turned his face towards Bhaskar and said, "Son, you go now and keep your spirit high. You have chosen the right path. The grace of God and the blessings of Acharya Ji are with you."

Bhaskar was totally speechless and the suspenseful conversation of the sage towards the sky was incomprehensible to him. He was in a state of awe when the sage urged him, "Don't spoil your time in attempting to untangle the ties knotted by the Supreme power. They are beyond human capabilities of comprehension. Go ahead with full trust and confidence."

Bhaskar felt as if he had woken up from a deep sleep. He touched the feet of the sage and walked to his bike. In a few moments, he was out of the sight of the sage who was still standing there keeping his hands folded towards the sky.

Cleaning the Cobwebs

Bhaskar reached home and narrated the abridged report of his journey to his parents. He told them that he reached Panna quite comfortably and met Shastri Ji residing at a place located in a forest-like area, and then returned safely. He also told them that he had a minor accident as his bike skidded on a bad road, as he knew it for sure that his father would have a minute observation of the bike. He concealed the incidents of his encounter with a tiger and the mysterious way of reaching Shastri Ji's location. He didn't mention the reference to the priest also. His mother was not interested in any discussion after knowing about the accident. She asked Bhaskar to take a bath, have lunch and take a rest. Bhaskar did accordingly and went to bed.

Bhaskar was lying in bed with his eyes closed but he was miles away from sleep. Multiple thoughts came rushing to him and he waited for the evening so he could go to the temple and meet the priest. He was perplexed by the Sage's hint of meeting the priest alone. Many questions circled his mind. *Is the priest hiding something? Could my father's presence affect the information? Is my father concealing some facts?*

As soon as the clock showed five in the evening, Bhaskar came out of his room saying, "Mother, I am going for a walk," and left the house. He walked briskly and thus, within half an hour, he reached the temple located in the centre of a clump, about one kilometre away from the border of the village.

He entered the temple premises as the small door within the main gate was open. There was complete silence. He went inside the main temple and also stamped the whole campus but observed nothing. So, he spoke loudly. "Is anyone here?"

He heard a thin voice. "Whosoever is there. I am in the backyard." He moved to the backside of the temple and found the priest brooming the floor. He greeted him with full respect.

The priest smiled and said, "Bhaskar! Son! Oh, it's you! Come." He gestured to him to sit on the platform circling an old Peepal tree. Bhaskar sat on it and after a while, the priest joined him.

The priest said, "Son, how did you come here today?"

Bhaskar, in a low voice, said, "Sir, I have come here with a few questions. Yesterday, I visited Panna and met Shastri Ji, who asked me to meet you in privacy. Actually, he advised me to meet you when my father is not nearby. May I know the facts which were concealed from me due to my father's presence?"

The face of the priest turned gloomy, and he said, "I stayed with Acharya Ji for six years in your house. However, I remained in contact till his last breath. Even after shifting myself from your house to this premises, I used to go to him daily for at least three to four hours."

Bhaskar's eyes widened with surprise, "But, you described things in a completely different way that day."

The priest said, "Son, don't take it otherwise, but I couldn't speak the truth in your father's presence as he instructed me to conceal a few incidents from everyone. I acted as per his will, but my conscience kept on throbbing inside. I told everything to Shastri Ji who had come to attend final rituals after Acharya Ji's demise. He also felt bad, but he asked me to follow your father's instructions. When I questioned him about the burden on my conscience, he said to me, 'Truth can be hidden for a while but cannot be destroyed. Don't panic unnecessarily. The truth will come out on its own when the time comes.'"

Bhaskar was stunned. He said, "And what was that truth?"

The priest said, "Acharya Ji took his last breath in my lap. He declared you to be the successor of his heritage. He said, *There is none in my family who deserves to hold the legacy I am leaving behind other than Bhaskar. Please tell him about that. Every belonging that is in this room should be kept intact. Everything that is in this room should be kept here only, untouched. Only Bhaskar should have the right to use these things, because only he can understand the real value of these things that may seem junk to others. Give my blessings to my child as I don't have enough time to wait for him. I have been asking my son for the last three days to bring Bhaskar from the boarding school, so that I can see him for the last time. But Bhaskar's father thinks that nothing will happen to me and calling Bhaskar home will only affect his studies. He wants his son to get education with one and only one purpose—getting a government job that holds enormous power and money. This is not the objective of education. A system that tends to produce positions cannot be said to be education. This is merely a business with no aims and objectives, having motives only. Education is about nurturing the natural talent of a child and simultaneously, training him to act in a socially approved manner and avoid deviant behaviour.*"

The priest stopped for a while on seeing tears rolling down Bhaskar's cheeks.

Bhaskar, with intermittent sobbing, said, "Please continue."

The priest said, "Son, that's all that I knew. I narrated everything exactly to your father. He, too, was very sad at his father's demise. He had a different perception of life than that of Acharya Ji, but it didn't affect the bond of a son towards his father. He carried out every wish of Acharya Ji, but was worried about you, so he tried to ensure that you should not get diverted from your main course of study. So, he instructed me to conceal the message from everyone, and not to reveal it to you till you get a good job. He was worried lest you follow your Dada Ji's way of life. But you shouldn't think badly about your father. He always respected his father and as per his wish, he kept his belongings with full care and maintained the room.

However, your father was also right as per his conception of life. The kind of financial difficulties he faced in his life compelled him to evaluate everything on the scale of monetary value."

Then, the priest said, with a serious note, "I seek your promise. Please never disclose to your father that I have communicated anything to you."

Bhaskar said, "You need not to worry. I will take care of it."

The priest said, "I owe your father for his numerous favours and help. I still feel that I cheated him by violating his instructions. But my conscience dominated my feeling of indebtedness and that's why I shared it with you."

Bhaskar greeted the priest and walked to the main gate. Suddenly, he heard the priest calling him, so he stopped and turned back towards him.

The priest said, "Once Acharya Ji told me that there are many people who always complain saying 'I should have done it earlier' or 'I should have got this opportunity earlier.' Unknowingly, they are challenging the cosmic itinerary decided by God. They need to understand that early or late is their own time frame which doesn't have any significance in the universal context. Everything occurs at its scheduled time."

Bhaskar nodded to him and then he walked home with a storm of thoughts. He thought that his father concealed the truth, but his motive was not to harm anyone. He rather acted in the interest of his son, whatever seemed correct to him. After a lot of brooding, he decided not to exhibit any signs of receiving the information from the priest and considered it to be sinful to make his father feel guilty. He felt very relaxed as he felt his clouded mind turning clear and the cumbersome burden of uncertainty took off from his conscience.

Breezing in the Boot Camp

He reached Gangotri early in the morning. He checked in a dormitory available near the bus stop and reached a hall with six mattresses spread on the floor. He put his shoes off and fell on a mattress. Within a few minutes, he fell asleep.

He woke up in a hurry and looked all around. There was none other than him in the room. He looked at his watch. It was 12:30 pm by the watch and he got annoyed at himself for sleeping so long. He took a bath and dressed quickly. He wore his backpack and started his journey to the address.

He asked the caretaker of the dormitory about the address. The caretaker told him that he was also new to the locality; he had arrived there only three days ago. He told Bhaskar that hardly fifty families resided in the place, so it wouldn't be difficult to find an address.

Bhaskar walked outside the dormitory and enquired an old man, coming towards him, about the address. The old man instantly directed him towards a point from where a narrow alley was descending and said, "Your destination will be one of those houses."

Bhaskar descended into the alley. He crossed a few houses and noticed an old lady sitting at the door of a house. He greeted her with full respect and enquired about the address. The lady instantly pointed her finger towards a house and said, "Yellow house, beside the tree."

Bhaskar moved quickly, expressing his thankfulness to the lady. He reached the house and stopped. He noticed an old copper name plate nailed on the wooden frame of the door displaying "Swami Vinayak Pandey."

Bhaskar got assured of the house owner's name. The door was open, but the curtain was spread. He knocked at the door and an instant reply came from inside. "Who is there?" The voice was essentially feminine.

Bhaskar replied, "I have come here to meet Swami Vinayak Pandey."

The feminine voice said, "He is not home."

Experiencing the intention of the voice source, to dispose of his visit so quickly, Bhaskar urged, "Ma'am, I have come all the way from Madhya Pradesh to meet Swami Ji. Will you please tell me at what time I can meet him?"

Bhaskar waited for a reply but there was no response. So, he again urged, "Ma'am, please tell me."

Suddenly, the curtain was drawn, and a beautiful girl appeared at the door. Bhaskar's eyes widened as he looked at the face of the girl. He turned speechless at the ravishing beauty of the girl. The girl was hardly twenty-one. She had a radiant look and a perfectly streamlined physique. She noticed Bhaskar's unblinking eyes but didn't get annoyed. Perhaps the girl was also impressed by his attractive personality and handsomeness.

She rather smiled and said, "Yes, who do you want to meet?"

Her voice was as mellifluous as the melodious sound of a chime. Bhaskar, now recovered from his state of enchanting awe, felt embarrassed by his stunned reaction. He greeted the girl very politely and said, "My name is Bhaskar Dixit. I have come here from a village located in Tikamgarh district of Madhya Pradesh. It is around a thousand kilometres away from here. Swami Vinayak Pandey was a disciple of my grandfather. I need some information from him."

The girl said, "OK, Swami Vinayak Pandey is my grandfather, but he no longer lives here."

Bhaskar's face turned dull with disappointment. He pleaded, "May you please give me his address. I am in dire need of meeting him. Please!"

The girl sympathised with him and invited him to come inside the house. Bhaskar stepped in and reached a room where an old-fashioned wire-woven sofa was placed with clean cushions on it. The girl requested him to sit there and went inside. The room was very neat and clean, having a single bed with a mattress covered by a clean white sheet in the other corner. There were a few framed photographs hung on the wall. The light fragrance of sandal incense was present in the room.

After a little while, the girl appeared and placed a tray with a glass of water before him. Just behind her, a middle-aged lady appeared from inside the house and sat on the bed. The girl introduced the lady as her mother, and Bhaskar greeted her.

The lady said, "My daughter Sanjana told me about you. Swami Vinayak Pandey is my father-in-law. He was the chief priest of Gangotri temple. Three years ago, he quit his position, then his son, i.e., my husband, was ordained as the chief priest. He himself relinquished the family and now lives in an ashram at Tapovan. Since then, we haven't seen him. My husband has managed to receive regular updates about his well being. He is in good health and relishing the peace and calm at the place. He experiences satisfaction by submitting himself fully through his devotion to God. Tapovan is not far away from here, but the passage to there is through extreme terrain. If you want to meet him, you must go there. However, I suggest you have a word with my husband. He is about to come home. May luck support you and you need not go to Tapovan if you get the desired information from my husband."

Sanjana appeared again, and this time with a cup of tea. Bhaskar took the cup and took a sip. The taste of the tea reminded him of the tea prepared by his mother.

Suddenly, a robust man of fair complexion, shaved head, wearing a big yellow mark on his forehead and attired in a saffron robe, came inside the house. In a nutshell, he was a monk with a magnificent personality. Bhaskar realised that he was the owner of the house and Sanjana's father. The monk was a little surprised to see a stranger in his house. The lady quickly introduced her husband to Bhaskar.

As a gesture of respect, Bhaskar stood up and greeted him with jointly folded hands. The lady then introduced Bhaskar to her husband.

The monk looked at Bhaskar for a while, sat on the sofa and said, "I am familiar with the grand personality of Acharya Ji. My father used to tell me about his scholastic achievements. You are privileged to be born in his lineage. However, your parents are privileged and fortunate to have a dynamic, handsome and lustrous son like you too. Please tell me. How can I help you?"

Bhaskar felt a little embarrassed by the monk's kind words. He lowered his eyes and then tried to gauge the reaction of others in the room. He observed the emotions of affection on the lady's face, while Sanjana's glaring eyes were accompanied with a serene smile.

He had already decided to conceal the actual reason for his arrival. With his innate quality of weaving brilliant stories, Bhaskar was ready to narrate a fictitious story.

He said, "A powerful and affluent family of our area was tempted to grab a piece of our agricultural land. The family runs multiple firms involved in construction, real estate and other similar businesses. They have strong political connections. A member of that family came to our house and insisted on selling that land to his firm, but my father politely declined his proposal. After that, they started pressurising and threatening us with dire consequences for not selling the land. My father made it clear that the land symbolised the bliss of our ancestors and thus cannot be sold at any cost. A few weeks later, we received an eviction notice from the local revenue office instructing us to vacate our possession of the land. We panicked and when we approached the revenue office, we came to know that those people had applied to get possession of that land. They have submitted a sale deed in support of their claim to be the real owners of the property and declared us usurpers. We were sure that the documents submitted were forged. Our lawyer also agreed that, however, the court will not decide the matter only on the basis of this document, but the sale deed is a significant document for claiming ownership. Thus, the case may remain pending for a long time, and it may take even ten to fifteen years for the final verdict to come. When we scrutinised the document closely, we found that the name of Swami Vinayak Pandey was recorded as one of the witnesses of the sale deed. Our lawyer has suggested that if Swami Ji makes a statement declaring that his name mentioned in the sale deed is false and his signature is forged, and such a deed never existed. In this scenario, the final verdict in the case will be made instantly. With this intention, I have come here to seek Swami Ji's help."

Hearing Bhaskar's words, all the three family members had expressions of sympathy on their faces. The woman looked at Bhaskar with great sympathy and said, "Son, God's mill grinds slow, but grinds very fine. No matter how powerful evil is, good is always mightier. God never allows injustice towards his true devotees. A lie always has some leaks, and those criminals will lose. Punishment in hell is fixed for those who mislead or harm others by telling lies."

Bhaskar felt the last sentence of the lady stinging in his heart. He realised that he, too, was lying. He had met the family just a few minutes ago, but for some reason he felt extremely guilty for having lied to them. He was ashamed of the depth of his heart. He was thinking, had he told the truth to them, at most, they would have laughed or considered him a fool, but at least, he would have been free from this self-reproach.

He took a vow in his heart that sooner or later, he would disclose the truth to them and explain the reason for his lie. He would also apologise to all of them for his act.

Bhaskar was lost in his own tumult of emotions, when the impressive voice of the monk brought him back to reality. He said, "Son, it is now clear that only my father can solve your problem and he will definitely help you. That means you will have to go to Tapovan. I think you have come here for the first time."

Bhaskar just nodded his head in the affirmative.

The monk said, "As you have come to Gangotri for the first time, then there is no question of having any familiarity with Tapovan. You should know that visiting Gaumukh or Tapovan requires a permit to be obtained from the district administration and the forest department. You can ride a mule up to Gaumukh, but from there you will have to trek and cross the glacier to reach Tapovan. You should understand that it will be a difficult journey and will put your stamina, strength and willpower to the test. Moreover, the season will aggravate your difficulties. Winter is about to come and within the next two weeks, the Gangotri temple will be closed for six months. The Vijayadashami festival will be held this week, so finding a navigator or guide will also be difficult. I would suggest you postpone your visit now and plan it for the month of April. Under the current circumstances, it would be better to return home now and come again in the month of April."

Bhaskar thanked the family for the support and assured them that he would embark on the journey only if the situation appeared normal. Bhaskar left the house, but some unknown emotion compelled him to feel sad on departing from the family. He wanted to turn around and see if Sanjana was at the door. For a long time, he held back the thought of looking back, but as soon as he saw the turn of the street, he realised that this would be the last chance to look back. After turning, he would not be able to have a glimpse of Sanjana's house. The thought broke his restraint, so he stopped instantly and looked back. Sanjana was still standing at the door and was watching him. As soon as Bhaskar turned around, Sanjana got embarrassed and pulled herself inside the house. The incident infused strange mixed feelings of romanticism, happiness and affinity into Bhaskar's heart.

The Faux Pas

Bhaskar reached the dormitory and enquired the caretaker of the facility about the process of acquiring a permit to visit Tapovan. He searched for a navigator but couldn't find any. He came to know that it would be very difficult to find a guide or a navigator at that point of time, because the winter had arrived and the temple would be closed for six months, within a week. So, with a little disappointment, he approached the local office and got the permit issued. Due to the unavailability of a navigator, his visit was authorised up to Gaumukh only.

He felt indecisive as he didn't have any interest in visiting Gaumukh. His primary objective was to reach Tapovan. He was in a tumult of thoughts and finally decided to take the journey. He decided to take a chance to go to the glacier terminus to look for the possibilities of moving beyond and reaching Tapovan without a permit. He knew well that journeying alone in unfamiliar and rugged terrain would be arduous and risky. But he consoled his reason by asserting that it was better to return from halfway than to sit at the initial point.

So, he collected all the essential information and planned to start his journey early in the morning. He returned to the dormitory and unfolded the maps that he had purchased from a shop. He was already good at geography and had an aptitude for map reading. He had managed to get a physical map, a topographical map, a climatic map, a thematic map of the geological features of the area and a navigational chart. He studied the maps very minutely. After deep observation and calculation for more than two hours, he found an alternative route. He assured himself that this route would skip the terminus of the glacier and the check post, as he had triple checked the details and cross-tallied the calculations from various available resources.

Bhaskar didn't have any interest in visiting the origin of the glacier and was only concerned about skipping the check post. He identified a spot around a mile before the glacier check post from where he would take the alternate route. He decided to follow the usual trail till that point. He thought over the pros and cons of every aspect and rechecked everything many times. After he was fully satisfied, he raised his arms above his shoulders and triumphed, "Yes!" He was happy to find a route that could get him rid of the requirement of a permit to Tapovan.

Bhaskar was merely a youth with very little worldly wisdom. He felt triumphant at cracking the monitoring system established to apply restraint on visitors. He laid himself on the mattress and started thinking about his efficiency to offer a solution to the problem within two hours. Then, he started to think that perhaps the pilgrims, the adventure tourists and those who worked there as guides or navigators weren't competent enough to find such a big gap in the route management. He also considered the local administration to be pathetic reviewers of the system. Bhaskar thought, "Had this route become public, the system of issuing permits would become senseless."

He felt extremely narcissistic at the moment. His idiosyncrasy made him forget what his father had told him many times.

"Confidence and overconfidence are only marginally apart. Till the time you think about your own abilities, you enjoy confidence and from the moment you start to focus on your superiority to others, you turn out to be a victim of overconfidence."

The Stepping Stones

Bhaskar started his journey very early in the morning by praying at the Gangotri temple. He took only essential things with him and left the remaining belongings packed in a plastic bag at the dormitory. He knew the importance of carrying the minimum possible luggage during a gruelling hike. He climbed the stairway to reach the trekking point and started walking along the trail. Within a few minutes, he reached the check post. He showed his permit to a security personnel who checked his bag for the plastics he was carrying.

During the formalities, Bhaskar sweet-talked with the security personnel in order to create a little affinity. He said, "Really, it's a strenuous task to work in such extreme terrain. You people are a brilliant example of dedication to duty." The personnel smiled.

Bhaskar said, "I am speaking from the depth of my heart. I salute your spirit of executing your duties despite so many adversities and difficulties."

The personnel now reciprocated his courtesy by nodding his head and gestured with his hand to express his thankfulness for the words of appreciation.

Bhaskar said, "I think I am not the first one to make such expressions. Everyone coming here must have similar feelings."

The statement provoked the security personnel to bring his agony to the surface and he said, "Not at all, brother. Many come here and quarrel, many turn rude and many of them think that we are wasting their time on useless formalities."

Bhaskar made a low sound by tightly joining his lips and then suddenly moving them apart, in order to show his sympathy. Despite knowing the locations of all the check posts on the route, Bhaskar said, "Perhaps this is the only check post on the route."

The security personnel told him, "No, there are two more; the last one is at Gaumukh. We are here to help people, but many people consider us foes. Once, a group of three boys insisted on the Gaumukh check post, allowing them to go further. Despite not having a permit to go beyond, they quarrelled with the staff and also manhandled one personnel. After returning from the check post, those boys took an abandoned track to reach Tapovan and lost their way. Two of them lost their lives and one survived anyhow, as the staff of the same check post rescued him."

Bhaskar was shocked and sad as well. He said, "The world is full of people with varied mentalities and outlooks. You please continue your good work." Then he exhibited a pleasant smile and said, "Now, I should continue trekking. Otherwise, I may lose the advantage of starting early. It was nice meeting you people." He waved to the staff at the check post and continued his journey.

Bhaskar had received two very significant inputs from the check post staff. First, it was possible to bypass the check post at the glacier and thus his plan of reaching Tapovan by skipping the check post and adopting an alternate route was quite feasible. Second, an alternative route could prove to be more hazardous than his assumption. He remembered what Baba Ji had told him about identifying the signs of destiny. He thought that the security person had mentioned the alternative route as the very sign to indicate a green signal to take the further course of his journey as per his plan. He was determined and proceeded with a stouter will.

The route was physically demanding, but Bhaskar's fitness and stamina came in handy. Bhaskar felt the need for his hiking shoes. While leaving home, he didn't anticipate facing such a situation, otherwise he could have packed his hiking shoes and other accessories. He conveyed thankfulness to his mother, who insisted on him carrying a heavy jacket and a balaclava. The initial span of the route was easy, and he continued his journey enjoying the soothing view of pine trees and vegetation.

Bhaskar was feeling comfortable as the trail was quite wide and he kept on walking on the left side of Bhagirathi River. He was amused by the beauty of the entire valley. He got a view of Sudarshan Peak and felt mesmerised on seeing a snow-capped mountain for the first time in his life. He crossed many streams along the way. His backpack was not heavy, so he could walk easily without needing to use his trekking pole. He was worried only about being alone in an unacquainted region with extreme survival conditions. After taking a single break, he saw a roadside facility and he realised that he had reached Chirbasa. It was 10 am by that time and he decided to stop for a cup of tea.

While having snacks and tea, he talked to the facility owner and got to know that he was the first trekker of the day and only a group of four people had crossed the facility yesterday. The man told him that they saw fewer tourists now as the winter was approaching and very soon the Gangotri temple would be closed for a period of six months.

He resumed his trek towards Bhojwasa which was still five kilometres away. He crossed the pine forest. He found that the trail was muddy with heterogeneous slopes. He also felt the gradual ascent along with the trail and decreasing tree line. After trekking for two hours through boulders and sedimentation, he found the valley to be widening and after a while he viewed a stretch of open land. He saw clumps of birch trees and then observed a few houses. That was Bhojwasa, the last settlement which could offer food and accommodation to the trekkers.

Bhaskar was panting now and feeling very low. It was 2 pm by then and he decided to take a halt and have some food at the place. He stopped at a small shop that offered local cuisine meals. He had lunch and then stretched his legs on the bench. He felt his body aching. Despite his firm determination, he felt his body screaming to give up for now. He felt exhausted and the dormitory available there was attracting him to walk in. He checked into an ashram that provided lodging and boarding facilities. He took a stretch on the mattress and felt as if his body had thousands of bones and each of them was aching. He felt his muscles vibrating on their own due to the strenuous work they did for the first time. Very soon, Bhaskar fell asleep.

Bhaskar woke up and found a staff member shaking him and asking for dinner. He realised that he had slept for more than six hours. He got up and felt his body cramping. He swallowed a painkiller tablet he had brought with him, and after getting freshened up, he took his dinner followed by a cup of tea. He was now feeling well. His brain started working and he focused his attention on the primary objective that had brought him there. He found that he was the only guest in the whole facility. He walked around the place and joined a group of staff members sitting around a campfire. He talked with them at length about the passage to Gaumukh and Tapovan. He grasped every input given by them with full attention. When he felt that he had received all the information and updates about the track, he left the group and went to bed.

A Saviour in the Maze

Bhaskar woke up quite early and prepared for the last stretch of the expedition. He knew that the glacier was not too far from there and he had to take extra care to conceal himself from the check post. He stepped outside the ashram and felt the chilling cold, but the beauty of the site holding a vast expanse of grassland in the lap of glorious mountains made him forget everything other than the sense of awe. Taking a few steps, he observed the magnificent Bhagirathi massif enveloped in fog and mist. He started trekking on the trail, which was gradually getting narrower. He had already decided to skip the check post at the glacier, so he was walking along the river. He planned to leave the main trail a little early and cross the glacier, taking a bigger round in order to leave the check post staff unaware of him. The trail was easy till the point from where he had decided to take a diversion.

While taking the diverted route, he realised that he was entering a totally unknown terrain just on the basis of information collected from limited resources. He was a little worried for a moment, but he persuaded himself to stay convinced of his plan by again verifying the route details from the map. He focused on his abilities, talent, willpower and chiefly his insatiable desire to embrace his destiny. He stood there for a while and made a brief prayer to the Almighty and his grandfather. Then, he turned towards the diverted route and kept trekking as per his plan. About two hours later, he observed a small glacial stream at a distance. He felt optimistic about the accuracy of the route selected by him.

Suddenly, he observed clouds gathering and it seemed that it would rain. Bhaskar kept his fingers crossed, praying to keep the rain away. He started walking fast because he realised that navigation along a glacier during rain would be a nightmare, even for professionals, and he was an amateur who had stamped in the terrain for the first time. It made him worried. The only thing that kept Bhaskar positive was that he knew the direction, and he was sure that he had remained attentive to it. Bhaskar kept on walking briskly but even after walking continuously for five hours since the morning, he was still in the maze of the glacier. The normal trail from Bhojwasa to Tapovan was six kilometres long and hardly took three hours, but he hadn't crossed the glacier yet. He felt his confidence ebbing to an all-time low, and a feeling of fear started to be cast on his mind. Moreover, low light made him lose his sense of direction and navigation. He tried to keep his mind cool and took a few deep breaths. Then, he calculated his path again and proceeded forward. He kept consoling himself that he might have missed the path, but he could still get a way out of this. He was walking fast and even after covering a long distance, he was still trapped in the labyrinth.

He stopped and looked all around; he felt the landscape moving gradually. At first, he considered it an illusion. But, very soon, he got scared when he found himself standing on a moraine. He felt a deep shiver tearing his body apart. He gathered his full strength and moved with caution to reach a still surface. His forehead was flushing with sweat, and he felt his garments wet from inside.

He started moving in a different direction and found an area full of boulders and rocks. He hopped, trying to get away from that scary site of sliding surfaces. Suddenly, he realised he had reached a dead end of the valley. He couldn't get ahead. There were steep ascents on the three sides. He turned hopeless and remembered the story of three boys told at the check post. He felt as if he had been thrown into an unmanned prison. He looked all around, but the vision seemed almost similar in all directions of the valley. He was already exhausted physically and now his mental abilities had ceased to even think of finding a solution. He was so scared that he lost his desire to fight against adversity. He surrendered and accepted that he had been unsuccessful. He realised that he would hardly survive for a few hours and now, he didn't have any energy or courage to pull himself out of this problem.

He recalled his mother and the deep love that she always poured on him. He recalled his father who sometimes seemed strict but always took care of his every need and requirement. He felt as if he was taking his last few breaths. It was for the first time that he had felt the scarcity of oxygen in the air. He felt giddy and took the support of a big rock and then groped a boulder to sit on it. After a while, he felt a little better and he raised his left hand to look at the watch which showed 4:30 pm. Bhaskar realised that he had been struggling in the labyrinth for more than eight hours.

At his wit's end, he realised that he had committed a faux pas by assessing the glacier to be an ordinary multicursal puzzle and thus he had questioned the craftsmanship of God. He also committed a blunder by overestimating his novice abilities and efficiency at par with those of experienced professionals. He felt his existence to be negligible before the creation of Nature. He started feeling the objects of Nature like mountains, rocks, sky, snow, air and almost everything, to be far more superior to his feeble body and primal intellect. He closed his eyes and accepted his approach as presumptuous. He prayed to God and apologised for rearing a self-conceit. He apprehended that his status in the universe was negligible, and his scanty competence was no match for the enigmatic mysteries of Nature. So, as a last resort, he submitted his existence to God.

Suddenly, Bhaskar heard a low sound of an unclear recitation. He considered it to be a hallucination. He heard a low but robust sound again, someone was reciting "Jay Shiv Shambhu." He turned his head towards the sound and observed an ascetic descending from a steep hill. He couldn't believe a person was descending such a steep hill with an ascent of nearly sixty degrees with such ease.

The ascetic moved briskly and in a rhythmic flow. He was rather waltzing and approaching quickly, holding a trident in his hand. The ascetic was almost naked, except for a rag covering his genitals. His body was smeared with ash, his matted dreadlocks were long enough to reach his waist and the matted tresses of his beard reached his navel. Bhaskar was astonished to see a man triumphing control over his senses in extreme weather conditions and temperature below freezing point.

He came near Bhaskar and stopped about a metre away. Bhaskar stood up and greeted him with his folded hands raised up to the level of his forehead. The ascetic reacted by raising his hand gesturing bliss. Bhaskar offered the ascetic to sit on the stone and he squatted on the pebbled ground. A small smile appeared on the ascetic's face for a moment. He took over Bhaskar's seat.

As soon as eye contact was established, Bhaskar felt a deep shiver. He stopped looking directly in the amber feline eyes of the ascetic.

The ascetic asked, "Where are you going, kid?"

Bhaskar replied, "Sire, I was heading to Tapovan, trekking all the way from Gangotri but lost my way, and thus roaming for more than nine hours within the glacier. I have not only lost the way to my destination, but also got trapped in the web of ice. You have appeared as if God has sent you to me."

The ascetic laughed boisterously, and Bhaskar felt as if the whole valley was laughing with him.

The ascetic then spoke in a very heavy voice. "God has more serious jobs to deal with. You cannot lose your way until you do not renounce your desire to reach the destination."

Bhaskar was very happy meeting the ascetic, as he saw a ray of hope to get out of this icy maze. Bhaskar said, "Sire, could you please guide me to find my current location?"

The ascetic asked, "Kid, how did you get here?"

Bhaskar replied, "Sire, I planned to navigate the glacier on my own and lost the way."

The Ascetic smiled and said, "What do you think, where are you?"

Bhaskar replied, "I think I am still near the glacier."

The ascetic replied, "Far and near are relative terms, having multiple meanings as per the situations. Their meanings are ever changing. I can say that the moon is near, but the sun is far away."

Bhaskar already had enough information about the behavioural traits and styles of sages, hermits and ascetics from the stories told by his mother. He remembered what his mother told him about Aghori ascetics. She told him that *'Aghori ascetics possess divine powers, but they present themselves with a macabre appearance and furious reactions.'* So, without getting even a little bit irritated, he continued to nod his head in affirmation and kept his folded hands together.

The ascetic continued, "This is an ephemeral trait that differentiates humans from other creatures. Despite knowing that such information is useless to bring any change in the circumstances, people crave to get more and more information and just make a pile of nonsense. Think, what will change if you come to know that your destination is half a mile away?

Instead of getting the measurement of distance, you should rather endeavour to confirm if you are on the right path."

Bhaskar shook his head and said, "Yes sire."

The ascetic appeared pleased with him and said, "One's etiquette and decency exhibit lineage; however, many fail to justify their inheritance as they consider heritage as a matter of the past, and past means obsolescence to them. But things are not so. The present is like the trunk of a tree, the future may be represented by foliage, flowers, fruits and other bounties. The roots of the tree are the ties of the past, however, not visible, yet important for the strength of the present and lucrativeness of the future."

Bhaskar said, "Yes sire, I firmly believe in the significance of the past in our present. That's why I am here to search for the ends of some loose threads, of the past, that are indicating signs of the future."

The ascetic smiled. "Signs and symbols are not easy to understand. People speak thousands of languages across the world. All of them have different symbols, different signs and different systems. But the sovereign power uses a totally different system of communication. This is the supreme system that does not need any language, any sensory ability or any other desirable requirement. It is universally appropriate to everyone."

Bhaskar was now feeling comfortable with the ascetic, so he added, "Yes sire, I think you are referring to the psychic unity of mankind."

The ascetic smiled in a mysterious way. Bhaskar felt as if the ascetic's smile was meant to ridicule him. The ascetic turned a little grave now and said, "Psychic unity tells us about the features that are common to a group, a kind of instinctive reaction that is common to all. I am talking about the method

God uses to communicate with everyone. You, too, are just seeking the meaning of the same."

Bhaskar was a little confused. He replied, "Me, sire? What?"

The ascetic replied graciously, "Dreams are the means of God's communication."

Bhaskar's eyes widened and his mouth opened in surprise. He wanted to speak but stammered, "Yes sire. How ... did ... you ... know? Exactly, it's a dream that brought me here."

The ascetic laughed and said, "A dream is merely a dream for fools only. Once you are awake, you cannot have dreams. But wise people do not let their dreams diminish. They transform their dreams into thoughts in their own language, because God gives you only dreams and no thoughts or ideas confined to a language."

Bhaskar was shivering with excitement and an outburst of emotions. He said, "Sire, how do you know about my dream? Please tell me its real meaning and purpose."

The ascetic smiled and put his right hand on Bhaskar's head, and said, "Your dreams are God's communication with you, specially designed and developed for you. None can disguise dreams as they make people realise their real attributes. Before God, everyone is equal, and it depends on the individual's affinity with God how clearly one can apprehend his language. Dreams reveal the real self without any artificiality, pretentiousness or ostentation. An evil person may fool others by wearing the robes of a sage but cannot have the dreams of a sage."

Bhaskar humbly asked the ascetic, "Sire, please reveal the truth of my dream."

The ascetic replied, "Kid, you are asking me to eat, to get your hunger quenched. Is it possible? When you start attaining the capability to enjoy the pains of a journey to reach your destination and start feeling the path as just an extension of the destination; when the path and the destination do not remain two separate entities; when you start feeling that your path and destination have got assimilated and unified, you should stay ensured that you are on the right path. Few things are ascribed to an individual, while many are to be earned. Achieving destiny cannot prolong your life, but it makes your acts immortal. This is your journey to seek God's motive behind the message you received. Be patient and make your efforts honestly."

Bhaskar kept silent. A deep distress and disappointment were apparent on his face.

The ascetic took a deep breath, stood up and stepped away, and then stopped. He turned around and said, "Think if a mother loses her patience to meet her child only six months after conception and gives birth to a premature baby. Was her decision appropriate and wise?"

Bhaskar remained silent but stood up and walked to the ascetic. In order to show reverence, he put his head on the bare feet of the ascetic.

The ascetic moved away saying, "Cross the ascent in front of you, that is the only thing between you and the place you need to visit now. May Lord Shiva bless you."

Bhaskar watched the ascetic walking away until he was lost in the descent. He was still mesmerised by the ascetic's appearance who had conferred on him a resurrection.

The Alchemist

He then moved towards the ascent and started climbing through loose rocks with caution as it was too steep. Within a few minutes, he finished the climb and saw a flat stretch of land with little vegetation. He guessed that he had reached Tapovan. He felt ecstatic. He ran towards the meadow but stopped just after a while. He was looking for the ashram, but he didn't notice any traces of a constructed structure. He was appalled at finding himself in no man's land. He looked all around but couldn't see anything. He knew for sure that the ashram at Tapovan had quite a large facility. He felt dismayed and started to walk forward. The sky had been cloudy throughout the day and daylight was diminishing quite quickly now. He was in such despair that he wished to cry.

He recalled his conversation with the ascetic, who had confirmed that his destination was just across the ascent. Bhaskar thought, "Can an ascetic lie?" Then he remembered that the ascetic had used different words. He strained his mind to remember the exact assertion of the ascetic.

Bhaskar was trying to remember the conversation when one more tribulation was inflicted on him in the form of rain from the sky. He realised that Nature was in a mood to aggravate the degree of his trials. He didn't consider it a good omen for him, as he didn't have a poncho or a raincoat. He forgot about the ascetic and realised that it would be his last night if he got wet in this severe bone-chilling cold. He started running in order to find shelter.

Out of the blue, he saw a dim light emanating from a distance, and he started sprinting towards that. He reached near the source in a trice and noticed a bunker-like low-heightened shelter made of stones that reminded him of the houses of the primaeval ages. The entrance was covered with an animal pelt.

He shouted, "Is anyone inside?" He got a quick response, "Come inside."

Bhaskar went inside and found a very old man sitting inside, near a small fireplace made with the help of pebbles. Bhaskar guessed that the old man must be more than eighty years old. The space was quite warm, and Bhaskar felt as if he had reached a heavenly abode. Bhaskar looked all around the room and saw a thick carpet made of rags spread on the floor and a low-height wooden stool. There was a wooden box in the corner with a glass bottle filled with oil being used as a lamp placed on it.

The old man said, "Take the stool and sit near the fire." Bhaskar obeyed him mechanically.

Bhaskar asked him, "Who are you, sir, and what are you doing here in this cold desert?"

Bhaskar observed clearly that the wrinkles on the face of the old man would elevate when he smiled. The old man said, "As per the tradition of hospitality, I should have asked you this question."

Bhaskar replied, "Sir, my name is Bhaskar. I hail from a small village in Madhya Pradesh. I was heading to Tapovan but lost my way and reached here."

The old man said, "Yes, I can understand, as only those who lost their way or who roam without a destination reach here."

Bhaskar said, "Does no one know about this place?"

"No one knows this place, people have only confusion about knowing," the old man said.

Bhaskar couldn't understand it clearly. He observed that the man started rotating his left hand behind a small heap of pebbles, and after leaning a little to his left and stretching his neck, Bhaskar saw a hand-operated air blower that was flaring the coals and a fire-red ball-like thing between the coals. "Sir, are you heating something."

The old man's eyes shrunk, and he said, "Kid, you seem naive as well as an unschooled boy."

Bhaskar felt humiliated but didn't say anything.

The old man said, "The expressions of humiliation on your face say that you are a well-educated boy, and you want to refute and resist my words, but the circumstances have kept you silent, as you cannot annoy the person who has given you shelter in dreadful weather in this desolate place. Am I right?"

Bhaskar stammered while speaking, he said, "No sir, there is nothing like that."

The old man wore a broad smile and said, "You are naive for sure."

Bhaskar didn't reply.

The old man said, "A masculine young boy with great energy and strength like you can throw this century-old man out of this place as a response to my impertinent remarks."

Bhaskar said, "No sir, I cannot even think of that, you have proved to be a saviour for me."

The old man said, "Even a baby can understand that if something is put on fire, then the purpose must be heating it. Perhaps you may want to know what I'm heating? Isn't it?"

"Yes sir, I meant the same," Bhaskar said with a smile.

The old man said, "You are a decent boy, so I need not tell a lie. I am making gold."

Bhaskar wasn't surprised, rather his face was glowing with happiness. He said, "OK sir, I got it."

"Your reaction does not seem normal. Most people would either be shocked, or they would have considered me a lunatic," said the old man.

Bhaskar said, "Sir, I am sure that you are speaking the truth."

The old man said, "How can you be so sure?"

Bhaskar replied, "Because your wooden box is a clone of that of my grandfather with the same label of 'Shree Laxmi Narayan' in identical engraving. People say he was also an alchemist."

The alchemist shrank his eyes, pouted his lips and remained silent for a while. Then, he said with a smile, "So, that is how you know what an alchemist is. What is the name of your grandfather?"

"Acharya Pushkar Dixit," replied Bhaskar.

"I have never met him, but I sense a kind of acquaintance with his name. If he possessed a box like this, it means he was also a member of the Alchemists Society. An alchemist is required to take on some responsibilities and is expected to follow some constraints. This world is mad for gold and people can kill others or can be killed by others for the sake of this precious metal," said the alchemist.

Bhaskar nodded to show that he agreed to the statement.

The alchemist continued, "Since time immemorial, history has been full of events that reflect men's temptation for gold. There have been many metals more valuable than gold, but none of them succeeded in replacing gold with the title of the most precious metal. Gold is precious for its scarcity, for its inertness, for its distinctiveness, and for the extrinsic value that people add to it. Gold is the only element available on the earth that remains pristine for centuries."

Bhaskar said, "Yes sir, I have also heard about the medicinal properties of gold."

The alchemist said, "Due to all these properties, gold has become a focal point of the human rush. It is for this reason that alchemists are expected to take special care so that they do not affect the harmony of society."

While speaking, the alchemist stopped abruptly, and then said, "Sorry kid, I forgot to offer you something to eat. You must be exhausted and hungry. However, I cannot provide you with regular food here, but I can fulfil the purpose for what people eat. You just pass that bag to me." The alchemist pointed at a corner.

Bhaskar kept sitting and stretched his body and hand to reach up to the corner, tried to pick up the bag, but felt the bag to be too heavy to lift with such a posture. So, he stood up, lifted the bag and handed it over to the alchemist.

The alchemist said with a gracious smile, "The whole world suffers with the same problem—if you are unable to do something, it doesn't mean that you are incapable, you rather need to change your position. A person standing on a plateau may think a flat ground to be a trench and a person at the bottom of a trench may consider the same ground to be a plateau. However, both are wrong. Once they reach the ground, only then do they realise the truth."

Then, the alchemist took out some bottles from his bag and drew a spoonful of powder from one of the bottles. He placed it on Bhaskar's palm and asked him to take it with water. Bhaskar took the powder. The alchemist then offered him a half spoonful of powder from another bottle. Bhaskar took it too.

After a few minutes, Bhaskar enthused about the effect of the powders he had taken. He said, "They are magical. I have read about magic potions in comic books. But they really exist, in powdered form. I feel like I have enough energy to reach home running and like I ate a fulfilling meal just a few minutes ago. What are these powders? These powders can revolutionise the world and can infuse a new life in the scope of medical sciences."

The alchemist turned serious and said, "They are magical because they are unknown. Neither are they rare nor are they common. You need to rise from the bottom of the trench and descend from the plateau in order to identify the reality. We have all heard the story of a farmer who reared a cow. He was very attached to his cow and took great care of it, used to give it good food, used to take it to the nearby river to bathe every day. After some time, his cow gave birth to a calf which was very weak. He decided to take good care of the calf as well. It was the first day of the birth of the calf and he had to take the cow to the river. He did not find it appropriate to take the cow alone to the river, leaving the calf behind. The distance to the river was long and the calf was feeble. Then an idea struck his mind, and he took the calf in his lap and took it along with the cow to the river and brought it back in the same way. Now it has become his daily routine. After a few months, the calf had become healthy, and its weight had increased manifold. But the farmer could lift the calf without any problem. After a few years, the calf grew into a healthy and huge bull and weighed several quintals. But the farmer was still able to lift that huge bull easily. Some people considered it a miracle, some considered it to be the effect of some magic potion, and some considered the farmer a practitioner of the occult. There is no magic in the world created by the Almighty. Our ignorance and the fear of the unknown create magic. The magic lies in our position of having the view and nothing else."

Bhaskar said, "Yes sir, you are correct. What I meant to say was that the knowledge about the ingredients of these powders can be beneficial for humanity."

One corner of the alchemist's lips quirked, he said, "Humanity is a sophisticated term for a large population of customers and knowledge is just a piece of information about the recipe for manufacturing a product in demand."

Bhaskar was shocked at the delineation of the bitter truth of society, primarily focused on financial gains.

Bhaskar wanted to say something, but the alchemist continued, "Thus it is better to let the world go as usual as it moves with the arrow of time. Have you ever thought about why Lord Vishnu incarnated as Rama or Krishna? He could have eradicated the existence of Ravana or Kansa in a moment, with his eternal and supreme power. But God offered the solution to the worldly problems as per the ways of the world that He created and furnished the rules of business in order to let the world move. Actually, magic is nothing, but knowledge known to very few. So, it is better to let the magic remain magic only. One endowed with some special privileges or powers or knowledge is bound to follow the eternal rules. The direction of the arrow of time in which the Universe moves is from order to chaos. The degree by which the order is distorted to chaos in a particular period is different to everyone. In human context, it is called life."

Bhaskar was completely silent and was listening to the alchemist with deep fascination.

The alchemist then drew a notebook out of his bag and handed it over to Bhaskar and said, "Open it and read the first page that contains the oath of an Alchemist."

Bhaskar went through the Oath, which reads as:

I do swear in the name of Shri Laxmi Narayan that I will bear true faith and allegiance to the Notions of Ras Vidya, as founded by Shri Nagarjun, and the Code of Alchemists, established by the Apex society, and that I will maintain the confidentiality and integrity of the branch even at the cost of my life.

I pledge that I will never

- *Reveal the secret of alchemy to anyone other than my baptised disciple.*
- *Reveal it to my baptised disciple until he attains an age of thirty years.*
- *Reveal it to my baptised disciple until he masters all the ten purgative methods.*
- *Reveal it to my baptised disciple until he has solemnly sworn/taken the oath.*
- *Exhibit or display the method publicly or before anyone other than my disciple.*
- *Make gold for my personal use or for my family.*

An Alchemist can make gold in the quantity specified only for the following purposes:

- *To demonstrate the method to a baptised disciple aged above thirty years. (Up to half Tola)*
- *Help the state in the event of war/epidemic. (Up to eleven Ser)*
- *To help the rebels of a state, for non-violent resistance, whose state is confiscated by foreign invaders. (Up to eleven Ser)*
- *To help the poor and needy. (Up to one Tola)*
- *To help someone in case of the abduction of one's wife/children. (As per discretion)*
- *To help a prodigy to pursue his career if the prodigy qualifies the test. (Up to seven Ser)*

Bhaskar closed the notebook and returned it to the alchemist, who took it back and kept it in his bag.

With a sigh the alchemist said, "But, we forget and fall. The temptation of wealth and status makes many degenerate, up to a level unfathomed. But always remember, the people who don't undergo any trials or tribulations in life are either deserters or renegers."

"So, does it mean that people who are happy are necessarily breachers?" asked Bhaskar.

The alchemist laughed briefly at his innocent question and said, "The answer may be yes or no, and it depends on your perception of happiness."

He paused for a while and then asked Bhaskar, "All the stories you have ever heard since your childhood are always about the trials, tribulations and ordeals of legendary figures and great people. Why is it so? On the contrary, the evil people enjoy their sensory pleasures throughout the story and get killed only in the end. Have you ever thought about it? Who is happy? One who underwent the hardships or the one who enjoyed the worldly pleasures? Compare the life of an ascetic who lives in the wild without any basic amenities and a person who lives in a big mansion in a town with all the advanced facilities. Who is happy? The answer may be different for two people if they have different perceptions."

Bhaskar said with full respect, "Sir, it is true that one's perception changes the way of looking at a certain aspect. But is there something like absolute perception? Is there a definition of absolute happiness?"

"Definitely, yes. Reality doesn't need any perception to be explained. What seems to be a physical or emotional torture may be a penance to reverse the arrow of time so that a soul can move from Chaos to Order. To experience absoluteness, one has to transcend this illusory world. If we talk in the context of worldly things, then, enjoying the state of being alive is absolute happiness. Similarly, developing your senses to identify reality is a state of absolute perception. But it requires rigorous discipline and practice," replied the alchemist.

Bhaskar was deeply impressed by the man's authoritative command on various subjects, and, above all, he was an alchemist. Such a great scholar's staying in the wild in primitive conditions with no ambition for materialistic achievements filled his heart with reverence for him. He said, "Sir, you are a great asset to society. Why do you stay here in such a forlorn place?"

The alchemist smiled and said, "Because I express indebtedness to God for giving me life that remains unchanged even in this barren land. I don't need anything else."

Bhaskar stood up and touched the feet of the alchemist and said, "It is God's grace that I got this opportunity to meet a great scholar and saint like you. I am fortunate."

The alchemist blessed him by putting his right hand on Bhaskar's head and said, "Listen carefully. The last thing that I need to tell you is that there is nothing like a bad situation or a good situation in the world. It's your perception of the outcome of the events that makes it good or bad. Perception is the result of your confidence and your trust in God. Whenever you find a situation that seems bad to you, endeavour to change your perception of the situation and you can deal with it easily with your abilities and the grace of God. These two always stay with you, but remember that only thinking will do nothing, you must act accordingly. Plans made on paper never work, their execution brings results and then you will find that no problem in the world is beyond your control."

Then he stood up and took two very thin blankets out of the wooden box and gave one of them to Bhaskar and said, "Kid, you should take a rest now. You may sleep here at this side of the fireplace."

Bhaskar took the blanket and found it to be very thin like a bed sheet, but it was quite warm. Then the man took some red coals and placed them outside, just near the entrance, and covered those coals with ash, and said, "These coals will keep predators away from us." Then the alchemist reached his place to sleep and turned out the lamp. They fell asleep soon after.

Taming the Nemesis

Bhaskar woke up to a beautiful morning. The sun was shining with glory. He looked at his watch and found that he slept till 9 am. He stood up in a hurry and then remembered the incident from last night. He looked for the alchemist, but he was not there, so he rushed outside and looked all around. He didn't find the man anywhere.

Suddenly, he remembered something and went inside quickly. There were no boxes in the place; only the pebbly fireplace was there with some signs of fire. He noticed a piece of paper weighed down with a small pebble and a small piece of gold.

He picked up the paper which read:

I didn't like the idea of disturbing you in your deep sleep and my pony was in a hurry to go. Keep the piece of metal with you and keep it safe for a while. It may prove to be miraculous in your world as it can turn your friends into foes, and similarly, make your foes treat you like friends. The glitter of this metal is so tempting that you can easily win favour, even from strangers, but keep yourself away from its tempting fervour. Enjoy the state of being alive and seek your destiny. Truly, life is an opportunity to reach destiny.

Lastly, it is quite normal to leave a few questions unanswered and sometimes it is essential.

The Alchemist

Bhaskar was totally puzzled. A variety of thoughts and questions were running through his mind. He was unable to think. In the meantime, he read the last line of the alchemist's message again, *"It is quite normal to leave a few questions unanswered and sometimes it is essential."*

He folded the blanket and kept it in his bag. He wrapped the piece of gold in paper and put it in one of his socks. He walked along in his journey and very soon found a steep descent. Suddenly, he observed a small meadow with a few tents camped at a distance. The sight filled him with joy and hope. He started descending slowly with caution. After a while, he safely reached down. Then he advanced in the direction of the camp site. Within half an hour, he reached there. He shouted for someone to reply. He felt some activity inside the tent, so he waited for someone to come out.

A man came out of the tent bearing expressions of surprise. He asked Bhaskar if he had come for the mountaineering expedition. Bhaskar told him that he had lost his way and wanted to reach Tapovan. The man offered him a cup of coffee and guided him on the way to Tapovan. Bhaskar felt energetic after having coffee and felt relieved by knowing the location of his destination.

He thanked the man and left for Tapovan. He was thinking about the last two days that had been very phenomenal for him. He kept walking through streams, boulders and loose rocks for around three hours when he saw a steep ascent. He was feeling tired, so he took a break. He put his bag on the ground and sat on a rock. He closed his eyes in order to relax.

Suddenly, he heard a sound of conversation. He looked in the direction and found four people descending from above. He observed that two of them had rifles hanging on their backs. Fear gripped his heart at the sight of men with guns. Bhaskar wished to hide from their sight, but it was not possible because they were not far away and there was no place to hide.

Bhaskar kept on sitting there, keeping his back towards them. He was already wearing a balaclava and now he wore his sunglasses too. The men descended soon, and they caught sight of him as he was sitting in the middle of their way. They came near him and one of them, wearing a holster with a pistol, asked, "Where are you going?"

Bhaskar replied, without turning his face towards them, "Tapovan."

The man asked him to show his permit. Bhaskar got scared and moved towards his bag. He reached for the bag and looked as if he was trying to find his permit.

Suddenly, the man with the revolver came to him, caught him with his neck and said, "Do you need any help in searching for the permit, Mr. Bhaskar Dixit."

Bhaskar felt as if he had been buried under a heavy rock. He was horrified and he wanted to fall at the feet of these people and beg to spare him. At that moment, he remembered the words of the alchemist that a man's skill and knowledge work only as long as he maintains his confidence and patience. *If you can do this, you can expect miracles.* Bhaskar decided to take a chance on the alchemist's lesson.

He quickly came up with a plan, turned towards the man and very calmly said, "Please don't involve guns." Then he took off his glasses and said, "It's not good to indulge in manhandling."

The man who turned out to be a security officer was not expecting such a reaction. He was taken aback by Bhaskar's impressive personality and his sombre reaction.

Bhaskar said very seriously, "Tell me, what do you want?"

The officer was still a bit surprised. He said in a loud voice, "You are Bhaskar Dixit. You were issued a permit for Gaumukh and that too, till yesterday. You did not even reach the Gaumukh check post and today you are trying to go to Tapovan illegally. We have to detain you."

Bhaskar's confidence was greatly increased by the changed tone of the officer. He smiled and said, "You know very well that you are not going to get any personal benefit by detaining me, and I am also not going to receive a death sentence. I am aware, that I have only broken a rule and that too, unintentionally, under adverse circumstances. I have not committed any crime or have been involved in any criminal offence. You will keep me in custody for at most one day, and then produce me before a court of law where I will submit my confession, asserting the motive and explaining the circumstances which led me to violate the rule. I know for sure that even in the worst scenario, the court will impose a maximum fine of a thousand rupees and will release me. It means that you are not going to get anything for all your efforts. Similarly, I shall be spoiling my two or three days and bear a financial loss of one thousand rupees. That means nothing is going to be phenomenal for either of us."

Bhaskar saw a slight glimpse of agreement on the faces of the officer and his subordinates.

That's why the officer said, "By the way, what was the reason for breaking the rules?"

Bhaskar sensed his plan turning out to be successful. He wore the expression of compassion instead of arrogant carelessness on his face. He leaned slowly and drew the blanket left by the alchemist for him out of his bag and said in a slightly emotional tone, "This is my grandfather's blanket." The appearance of the archaic blanket left no scope for anyone to doubt.

Bhaskar continued, "He spent a major part of his life here in Tapovan and his last wish was to make one last visit to the place, but his sudden demise resulted in his last wish being unfulfilled. A religious scholar suggested that I should leave his shawl at Tapovan as a symbol of his affinity with this place. The scholar said that this ritual would confer salvation on the departed soul. I came here with this objective only. I applied for a permit to visit Tapovan, but without a navigator, I was issued a permit up to Gaumukh only. I had already tried my best to find a guide or a navigator, but due to the last days of the season, I could not find any. Then, I decided to go to Tapovan without a permit. Had I left my grandfather's shawl in Gaumukh instead of Tapovan, would my grandfather's soul have found peace? Moreover, I would have remained plagued by the guilt of my act for the rest of my life."

Bhaskar was demonstrating himself, to be very emotional. He stood for a while and remained silent. In the meantime, one of the security persons said to his colleagues, "Yes, he is right; I have noticed many hermits in Tapovan using exactly similar shawls."

His statement seemed an added advantage to Bhaskar, and he said with great confidence, "If you take me today, I will come again. I must go to Tapovan at any cost."

All four people were stunned. Bhaskar realised that his plan had worked. Then he smiled and said, "I have another option as well. If you allow me to go to Tapovan, I will give you a small gift."

Bhaskar deliberately added a few more sentences. "Once I perform the ritual for fulfilling my grandfather's last wish, I will turn up before you and then I will gladly accept any punishment you decide appropriate."

The security officer said a little softly, "Bhaskar Ji, we are also human beings, we respect your feelings. But we also have to do our duty."

Bhaskar was quite happy as he successfully tackled the situation. He said, "Yes, I can understand. I had a bad time too. I left Bhojwasa yesterday morning, lost my way in the glacier and reached Nandanvan at night. I spent the night there in these clothes only. It was only because of my grandfather's blessings that I met a member of a mountaineering squad who helped me to reach here safely."

Bhaskar paused for a while and then said, "I can understand that my mistake has troubled you a lot. I am really sorry for that." Then he leaned and removed the paper packet out of one of his socks. While uncovering the packet, he said, "I have a small gift for you to express my regrets." And then, he uncovered the glittering piece of gold and said, "One tola of twenty-four karat gold, please accept it."

The gold filled the eyes of the members of the squad with temptation and happiness.

Bhaskar, with a little force, handed over the piece of gold in the hand of the officer and said again, "Please accept it, otherwise my feelings of regret will never go away."

The security officer kept the piece of gold in his pocket and said, "Don't worry Mr. Bhaskar. You can go to Tapovan with full freedom and complete the ritual for your grandfather. I will shut the case today only. I will call any registered navigation guide to my office and get his signature as your navigator in the official records. I will submit my investigation report stating that the whole case was just a result of erroneous record keeping."

Bhaskar said, "Thank you very much, sir." Then, with great humility, he said, "May I ask you to please help me a little more."

The security officer said with great affinity, "Please tell me."

Bhaskar said, "Sir, tomorrow I shall return from Tapovan, and I think that security persons deployed at the check posts will enquire again on the same issue of validity of permit. May you help me in this matter?"

The security officer said with a smile, "You don't worry about that at all. You show me your permit." Bhaskar took out his permit from the bag and gave it to him. The officer wrote something on the permit and said, "Take this, I have extended the validity of your permit for two more days and modified the details of the area to be visited. I have put my signature below the revised details and mentioned my name. All these check posts fall under the purview of my authority and thus all the staff deployed there are my subordinates. Even if you come across a patrolling squad, they will be the people who work under my direct control. So, you need not worry about anyone. You just tell them that the Area Officer, Mr. Mathur issued the permit manually after modifying the area details and revising the period of validity. Then no one will question you. Even if any problem arises, feel free to tell the concerned person that you are a family friend of Mr. Mathur and the same can be verified by contacting him on radio."

Then, the officer put his hand around Bhaskar's shoulders and gently made him turn his back towards his subordinates. Then, he, along with Bhaskar, started walking away slowly from the three guards. The officer, without any hesitation, whispered in Bhaskar's ear, "You can see those two police constables and a forest guard. They have also been working hard since last evening. They are all paid very small amounts as salary. I advise you to offer each of them one thousand rupees, so that they may forget their tiredness."

Bhaskar realised that the officer was very cunning and corrupt, but he couldn't risk denying his demand as it could spoil his whole plan. However, he was worried about the availability of funds, as he knew clearly that he had only four thousand rupees left with him. He took out his wallet and handed over three thousand rupees to the officer.

The Officer loudly said, "Mr. Bhaskar, don't take it otherwise. I don't need this money. You please hand over the amount to them with your own hands." The officer then called the three guards and gestured to them to receive the amount. Bhaskar gave one thousand rupees to each of them.

Bhaskar thanked them again and took leave of them. He proceeded towards the steep ascent. After dealing with the Area Officer, his confidence was at cloud nine and he was finding the difficult climb very easy. At the same time, he was also worried about the shortage of funds, as he realised that the amount left with him would not be enough for his return journey. But he decided not to ponder the issue of funds at the moment and to deal with the problem later.

Only then did he realise that had the fortuity of meeting the alchemist did not occur the previous night, he would not have survived in a temperature below freezing point, and even if he had somehow survived, it would not have been so easy to handle the cunning security officer without the things left by the alchemist.

Then he sensed that perhaps the alchemist already knew everything and that was why he left his blanket and the piece of gold. It was also the alchemist's advice, exhorted with great emphasis, which infused him with the firm determination to handle the security officer in a different manner. Bhaskar realised that everything that the alchemist had said had proved to be true. It was his written message that triggered his mind to offer the piece of gold in order to win the favour of the security officer. Had he not met the alchemist, he would have been either in heaven or in police custody. Was the alchemist just there for him?

Getting to the Oasis

Bhaskar was climbing at a good pace and suddenly he caught sight of a vast expanse of open land. He pushed himself with all his strength to get a complete view as soon as possible. Then, he got the full view and found it to be a vast meadow with ample plain ground, with scattered bushes, boulders and a freshwater stream. The view was magnificent and amazing, taking his heart away. Then, he looked all around and experienced a glorious view of Mount Shivling, Mount Meru, Mount Sumeru and the Bhagirathi peaks from this high-altitude meadow. He explored the valley with the temptation of witnessing the maximum elegance possible.

He could also easily see the ashram. He moved gradually towards the ashram gate and saw the "Rules for Visitors" displayed prominently on the front wall. He went inside to meet the caretaker and deposited the amount in advance to avail the facility for lodging and meals. He couldn't find the caretaker. A volunteer told him that the caretaker would be back after some time, and he could check into the dormitory and use the facilities instantly and the amount could be deposited afterwards. Bhaskar looked at his watch. It was two o'clock in the afternoon. He had been in a disoriented state for two consecutive days. He took out a towel from his bag and headed towards the washroom. He freshened up, took a bath and changed his clothes. Now he was feeling well. The hot water bath had removed his tiredness to a great extent. He got ready and headed to the kitchen of the ashram. He again requested a volunteer to assist him deposit the amount against the charges for his stay and meals.

The volunteer told him that the caretaker wasn't back, so he could have his lunch first and complete the formalities later. He went to the kitchen and requested food. The volunteer in the kitchen offered him a meal with great affection. After finishing the meal, Bhaskar realised that he was very hungry. After being satiated, he started exploring the ashram and had an overview of the whole ashram. He realised that all the volunteers of the ashram gave as much support and service to the visitors as possible. He had feelings of respect for them. He also realised that everyone had immense respect for Swami Ji.

In the meantime, the kitchen volunteer offered him tea. Bhaskar went with him and sat near a stove in the kitchen and sipped his tea with those volunteers. Bhaskar felt that drinking tea while sitting with them generated a kind of affinity. Then a round of discussion started. Talking to them, he came to know that apart from the ashram, there were many known and unknown natural shelters in the area where many sages and hermits still practised meditation and penance. Many sages and ascetics left the place and shifted to other places deep in the Himalayas after regular people started flocking to this place. He also came to know that Swami Ji had a reputation as a highly spiritually enlightened sage, and the ashram was just a base camp for him. He frequently left for unknown remote places located deep in the valley for his spiritual practice. Swami Ji wanted to lead a life of complete celibacy and renunciation, but on the request of the saints and the trust of the ashram, he stayed as a patron and guide of the ashram. A separate room was reserved for Swami Ji, but he had only a mat and two boxes there. He used the room only to avoid disturbance by people.

Bhaskar also came to know that a joint squad of the forest and police department had come to the ashram looking for a youth who had been missing for two days. That young man had a permit only up to the glacier. He left Bhojwasa yesterday morning but did not reach the glacier check post till late evening. A group of climbers who were observing the valley through binoculars, informed the check post that they had seen a young man crossing the glacier.

All the volunteers were calling that young man a crazy person, devoid of any concern about himself and his family. Bhaskar was enjoying their discussion, realising that none of them knew that they were sitting with the same young man. Bhaskar felt like telling the truth but couldn't summon the courage to speak. Then, Bhaskar asked them about the details of the young man but none of them were aware. However, one of the volunteers informed them that the search team had provided the details of the young man to the caretaker.

Now Bhaskar realised that he had to tell the truth. So, he revealed to them that the young man they were talking about was sitting with them. Everyone was shocked to learn the truth. Bhaskar explained that he had already met the search party before reaching the ashram and all the confusion occurred only because his permit was amended manually after being issued and the concerned officer had not updated it in the office records. He also showed the permit to the volunteers. Bhaskar's explanation was so precise that those who were calling him crazy before were now calling the government officials fools for creating a mess. After having a long discussion, they dispersed.

A fresh meal and a hot cup of tea restored Bhaskar's energy and he was turning impatient to meet Swami Ji. He was afraid lest Swami Ji should return to the ashram. So, in order to divert his attention from these perplexing thoughts, he went for an outing. The weather was typical Himalayan glacial weather, with chilling wind gushing at moderate speed and the temperature below freezing point. He walked up to a short distance, finding his clothes insufficient for the conditions prevailing in the terrain. He watched the spectacular beauty of the mountains capped with snow, the flat stretched meadow, the gorgeous stream seeming descending from the sky and the foggy valley narrating the mystical gospel of Nature. But it was for the first time in the last four days that he felt the weather to be harsher than his tolerance. So, he decided to go back to the ashram. When he returned, he found that the caretaker had arrived. So, he approached the caretaker to deposit the amount against the facility charges for stay and meals. He was expecting the caretaker to be stunned on knowing his name, so, he submitted his permit along with the amount to be deposited. As the caretaker had already received the full information about him from the volunteers, Bhaskar was not required to explain the issue. The caretaker offered him a welcome and told him that he could stay anywhere in the dormitory as he was the only guest of the day. The caretaker expressed the possibility of Swami Ji coming back soon.

Suddenly, a lean and thin person in a saffron robe entered the premises. His head and his face were shaved, his skin was taut and glowing, but his snow-white eyebrows indicated his super-seniority of age. The caretaker stood up from his chair and a volunteer ran ahead of him to open his room. The caretaker whispered, "Swami Ji has arrived." Bhaskar too, stood up from his chair and offered respectful greetings by raising his joined hands up to the level of his head. Swami Ji stopped for a split moment, looked at Bhaskar, smiled and then proceeded towards his room. Bhaskar's happiness knew no limits on finding Swami Ji back in the ashram.

Bhaskar asked the caretaker whether he could go to Swami Ji's room and meet him.

The caretaker replied by shaking his head in negation and said, "He will call you, if he wishes."

Bhaskar again emphasised the urgency of his meeting and requested the caretaker to at least communicate his name and details to the sage, so that he might know Bhaskar's purpose of visit. The caretaker smiled and said that Swami Ji did not require any details and would meet him if the matter was urgent. Bhaskar couldn't understand what the caretaker meant. So, he kept silent.

Only then did he see a volunteer approaching him, who told him that Swami Ji had called him. He was surprised and he could see the caretaker smiling.

Bhaskar went along with the volunteer who stopped at the gate and asked him to go inside. Bhaskar entered the room, which had a mat spread on the floor, a wooden box in the corner with a bag on it and a robe hanging on the wall. Swami Ji was sitting on the mat, and he asked Bhaskar to accompany him. Bhaskar prostrated before Swami Ji and then sat before him.

Swami Ji wore a pleasant smile on his face and said, "Now your journey has started turning fruitful as you are acquiring worldly wisdom very quickly." Bhaskar said, "Sir, if you think so, it must be true. However, I came here with only one purpose of meeting you."

Swami Ji said, "Don't you think the way you tackled the shrewd Area Officer was no easy task, even for a seasoned man having vast experience of different walks of life?"

Bhaskar couldn't speak a single word in surprise and astonishment.

Swami Ji continued, "You had that exceptional talent of telling stories since your childhood. Acharya Ji himself was highly influenced by your skill of weaving perfect tales at the age of five. He communicated it to me also."

Bhaskar said, "But I told a lie to those officers in order to continue my journey uninterrupted and spare detention."

Swami Ji said, "I cannot justify you. But the phenomenon of telling lies can be classified in multiple categories. Lord Krishna has said that speaking the truth is indeed a great virtue and perhaps no other virtue is superior to speaking the truth, but the practical aspects of speaking truth are very difficult to understand. It takes a lot of time and maturity to understand the real nature of truth. If a lie spoken is detrimental to another person or has brought some undeserving benefits to the speaker, then it is unacceptable. You must have heard the story of Kaushik, whose truth resulted in a massacre of villagers. So, Kaushik was thrown into hell for speaking the truth. Kaushik is remembered for his foolishness and not for his vow to speak the truth."

Bhaskar felt a little relieved and then he said, "Swami Ji, as you are aware of everything, I request you to please enlighten me on the message that my Dada Ji wants to communicate."

A broad smile appeared on Swami Ji's face, he said, "Acharya Ji's was a complete personality with a divine blend of knowledge, skills, logic and intellect. His knowledge was imbued with deep research and sublime experience, while his skills exhibited the masterly efficiency gained through the hard work and practice of decades. His wisdom reflected the discretion to sense the merits and demerits of anything on the sound basis of his deep insight, keen observation, moral integrity and a clear understanding of religious faiths, norms and values. His arguments used to be precise and sharp, containing facts and references derived from an in-depth analysis of natural and supernatural phenomena. The dimensions of his knowledge were so vast that the scope of knowledge itself seemed limited before him. You do not need anyone else's help to understand his message. He didn't want to give any message, but he wished to give you the ability to choose the right direction on the path of your destiny, and also wished to ensure that no problem should hinder your way. He wished that if you exhibit determination to achieve your destiny, then you should be provided an opportunity to make choices with your own intuition. Let no circumstance or circumstantial obstacle distract you or affect your power of volition."

Bhaskar was listening to Swami Ji with full attention and interest. He said, "Swami Ji, I have been unfortunate as he departed when I was just eight. Had he remained for a few more years, I could have learned many things from him."

Swami Ji asked Bhaskar, "Do you know about Acharya Ji's teacher who helped him attain excellence?"

Bhaskar seemed very curious, and he said, "No, Swami Ji, I don't know anything about him. I am not even familiar with his name. Please tell me."

Swami Ji smiled. "Acharya Ji himself was his teacher. He attained all the knowledge by his own efforts. However, he considered Shri Laxmi Narayan as his symbolic teacher, yet no human ever taught him. So never feel sad about his demise, as he departed at the moment already scheduled for his exit. You should rather feel happy about being lucky to receive his manifest presence for eight years and his blessings have always been with you and will remain forever."

Bhaskar was getting emotional, and his eyes were getting misty. Swami Ji could feel his inner turmoil, so he asked Bhaskar to drag the wooden box placed in the corner to him. Bhaskar did accordingly. Swami Ji opened the box and took some papers out of it.

He handed over the papers to Bhaskar and said, "This was the last letter that I received from him. Go through it and you will be able to understand many things."

The letter read:

Dear Vinayak,

I am scribing this letter to you as you are the only one who is truly aware of the objective I follow. I am sad to foresee that society is moving through a transition and the dawn of the new era is impending. Few people think that I am an altruist. But it's not true. I have kept my conscience away from temptations, but today I observed my grandson's prodigious talent, and thus cannot block my tempting wish to confer a memento on him.

I am afraid that in this new era, talents will not be able to remain altruistic, as growing materialism has already altered the definitions of every concept. Following a unidirectional route in pursuit of pure knowledge will become an esoteric path very soon and the world will be dominated by charlatans practising pseudo-sciences.

Thus, I can clearly assume that this prodigy may also fall victim to the mentality of materialism. I wish that an excellent sapling should be given full opportunity to grow, strengthen and expand. But I am afraid that a plant having the potential to grow into a huge tree could be suppressed to remain a bonsai and may be turned into a potted tree with a shiny vase having only conspicuous value. The prospects of producing a harvest will be smothered in the bud.

You need to guide him to invoke his inherent traits in order to enable him to hold the heritage established by ancient Indian masters, and to receive the legacy entrusted only to him. This legacy will help him to remain protected from the contiguous disease of materialism. It had been a tactic of ancient Indian physicians to develop immunity against venoms and poisons in the key members of the royal families by turning them venomous. Only venom can make venom ineffective. Similarly, wealth can make the effect of materialism recessive.

You need to guide him, to make him realise that the belongings of his grandfather are not useless. I know that after me, my books, notes and consumables will be left abandoned, but you need to sensitise him so that he agrees to observe all my belongings. Prima facie, it is quite possible to consider books as obsolete or useless. But I am sure that once he catches sight of Rasas, he will get his interest aroused. The lucid flow and brilliant glow of mercury has always attracted me. While writing this letter, I am still mesmerised by looking at a half litre glass bottle, holding seven Ser of mercury. Even at the age of eighty, my passion is so young that I keep it and other Rasas in a locked almirah in my room. Anyone may consider me an old fanatic because of this.

Thus, I insist you enlighten the kid with the fact that his grandfather's belongings are not junk and if he observes them with a purpose, this junk can endow him with the capability to pursue his interest and passion. Tell him that his grandfather has remained a poor fellow throughout his life, willingly and by choice. He is the only one to whom I entrust my legacy, so that he can hold the heritage.

You are already aware of my involvement in the freedom struggle of the country. I, along with the fraternity of freedom fighters, used to work in central India, and Birla house in Delhi was the centre of our activities. We were all witnesses of the construction of Shree Laxmi Narayan Temple, also known as Birla Temple.

So finally, I expect that you should convince him to at least go to Birla Temple as priority, not only to have the darshan of Shri Laxmi Narayan, but also to visit the whole premises of the temple. I am sure that God will guide him to embark on a journey on the path destined for him. He can feel a divine consciousness in everything present there. Guide him to observe all the wall paintings, inscriptions and moral lessons, so that he may feel the consciousness completely and may pursue his interests without having any worries.

Yours,
Pushkar Dixit

Swami Ji said, "This letter has remained an enigma to me for the last twenty years, as many things have seemed obscure to me. However, it was not typical of the writing style of Acharya Ji. I brooded for weeks to find the meaning in those parts but remained unable to grasp it. Finally, I thought perhaps Acharya Ji was very desperate in his last days and was under heavy emotional turbulence. It was for this reason that he became obscure in expressing his inner state."

Swami Ji continued, "Around twenty days after receiving this letter, I received a parcel from him containing five grams of pure gold with instructions to pay you an amount in cash equivalent to the value of the piece of gold. It was mentioned that the amount being paid is specifically for the purpose of meeting the expenses to be incurred for your visit to Birla Temple of Delhi. The parcel also contained a sealed envelope with a letter inside it. The letter was addressed to you with a clear instruction that the letter should be handed over to you if, and only if, you swear not to open it till you complete your visit to Birla Temple."

Bhaskar was listening cluelessly to Swami Ji.

Swami Ji said, "This is all that I have. It has been more than two hours. You may go and have dinner. We will talk after that."

Bhaskar stood up, greeted Swami Ji and left the room.

The Glory of the Past

Bhaskar too, like Swami Ji, didn't understand the letter wholly. But he got a clear idea that his Dada Ji held him in high esteem and had a great affection for him. He also realised that the intellectual and spiritual level of his grandfather was much higher than his conception. He felt proud to be his grandson. The volunteers of the ashram also considered him special as they had never seen Swami Ji spending such a long time with anyone. Bhaskar felt the change in the attitude of the volunteers too. Those who exhibited affinity with him initially were paying great respect to him now. They offered him dinner and a cup of tea after the meal without his demand.

Bhaskar had his dinner and got a seat near the fireplace installed into the lobby. Only then, Swami Ji came in the lobby and everyone sitting there stood up as a symbol of respect to him. Swami Ji came near Bhaskar, gave him a shawl and asked him very affectionately to follow him. He walked out of the ashram and Bhaskar followed him silently. As soon as Swami Ji reached the main gate, he asked Bhaskar to wrap the shawl around him. Swami Ji himself was wearing only a cotton robe. He said, "You are not accustomed to going for a walk-in temperatures below freezing point, so take the necessary care to avoid adverse effects of cold in this frigid meadow." Bhaskar obeyed him and walked out of the ashram with him.

Swami Ji led him to the edge of the meadow and asked him to observe the sky full of twinkling stars. Bhaskar got a spectacular view of the starry sky with a clear view of the milky way core.

Swami Ji pointed towards the horizon in the north and asked him, "Do you know that star?"

Bhaskar said, "Yes, that is the Pole star or Dhruva Tara."

Swami Ji said, "Are you aware of the legend of Dhruva?"

Bhaskar said, "Yes."

Bhaskar wanted to speak more, but Swami Ji interrupted him, asking, "And the modern scientific theory about the Pole Star?"

Bhaskar said, "Yes, in ancient Indian scriptures, more specifically, in Puranas, we come across the story of Dhruva, a prince who did severe penance and was assigned the exalted position of the fixed Pole Star by Lord Vishnu. It is also worth mentioning that it points us to the geographic north and is aligned with the Earth's axis of rotation. It is positioned as it will be just above the viewer's head, if viewed from the North Pole."

Swami Ji smiled and said, "Very good. Dhruva also occupies a very important place in traditional Hindu marriages. A bride is asked to look at the Pole Star to derive inspiration to stay firm and strong in her new journey of life. Dhruva is one of the most popular and inspirational legendary figures in children's stories too. Every child evolves a curiosity to see Dhruva and he is usually shown the star Polaris to be the legendary star."

Swami Ji continued, "But, do you know that the star which is described as Pole Star or Dhruva Tara in our Puranas and other scriptures is not the star Polaris that people usually consider as Dhruva? At that time, Beta Ursa Minor was the Pole Star, while today we see Alpha Ursa Minor in that position. Modern astronomy has found these things recently, but our ancestors knew it thousands of years ago. Even I knew it before modern astronomers, as Acharya Ji explained the concept to me around fifty years ago."

Bhaskar was listening in awe.

Swami Ji continued, "Look at Saptarshi Mandal or The Great Bear. Focus on the penultimate star towards the tail. In South India, it is an old tradition in Hindu marriages that the bride and the groom are asked to look at this star just after their marriage. This star is called Vashishtha; western astronomers call it Mizar. So, what was the purpose of showing this star to a married couple? Our ancient scholars knew that it is not a single star, but they are two stars. It is rather a unique binary star system in which both the stars revolve around each other, and we named the stars Vashishtha and Arundhati. Arundhati was sage Vashishtha's wife. So now, the motive is clear that it aimed at developing an understanding in the couple, that a relationship between a husband and wife should be akin to twin stars and their lives should revolve around each other in propinquity, having both as the mutual centres for each other, thus any possibility of collision should be ruled out."

Bhaskar was mesmerised and amazed by the depth of the knowledge of the ascetic. He thought, had an academician of the modern world possessed even a split part of Swami Ji's knowledge, he would have proclaimed himself the status of a polymath having mastery in every discipline.

Swami Ji said, "My purpose of telling you all these titbits about astronomy is not to influence you with my knowledge or to motivate you to pursue your career in astronomy. I rather aim at telling you that the feeling of self-pride is the supreme happiness, and we have the privilege of having such glory. Our ancestors knew thousands of years ago that Antares is the biggest thing in the sky and that's why they called it Jyeshtha. They calculated the speed of light in an era when the rest of the world was pursuing a primitive life. So, develop a sense of glory in your past, and feel privileged to be a bearer of a rich heritage. Choose what you want to do, what you are good at, what strengthens your competence, what unifies your temperament and abilities, and what makes you feel relaxed. If you choose your area of interest as your profession, you will never feel exhausted."

Bhaskar said, "Yes sir, I promise you, rather, I solemnly affirm that I will devote my life to the purpose of preserving the heritage that has been kept, enhanced and advanced by people like my grandfather and you." Bhaskar's face seemed to be glowing with the halo of his vow and the robustness of his commitment.

Swami Ji had a feeling of satisfaction on his face. He said, "It is quite late now. You have to trek tomorrow, so you need a good sleep tonight. Let's go back." And he walked back to the ashram and Bhaskar followed him silently.

Bidding Adieu

Bhaskar woke up to a chilling morning. It was nine o'clock and he left bed hastily. He never slept till so late in the morning. He rushed towards the washroom and within twenty minutes, he was ready to take on the new day. He went to the lobby and a volunteer offered him tea and breakfast. While having his breakfast, he came to know that Swami Ji was in meditation. He was also told that Swami Ji had assigned a volunteer to accompany him up to Bhojwasa. Only then did a volunteer come to him and introduced himself as the person assigned the duty to guide him the way to Bhojwasa. The volunteer suggested that it would be better to leave as early as possible because he had to return to the ashram before night.

Bhaskar realised the importance of his advice and quickly finished his breakfast and got ready to leave. Then, he went to meet Swami Ji to bid him farewell. Swami Ji handed him an envelope containing some cash and another sealed envelope inside.

Swami Ji said, "One envelope contains an amount equivalent to the value of five grams of gold which will be more than sufficient for the expenses of your journey to Birla temple. The second envelope is a letter addressed to you, but you must swear that you will open it only after you complete your visit to the temple."

Bhaskar swore the same and then prostrated before Swami Ji as an expression of respect to him. Swami Ji blessed him and said with a mystical smile, "Once you get this matter resolved,

I think you should visit Gangotri once more. You still have a pending commitment. You need to tell Sanjana the truth of the story that you narrated there."

Bhaskar's face flushed with a red tinge as a mixture of strong embarrassment and discomforting shyness. He just said, "Yes sir, I will definitely meet your family and share the truth along with my reservations about concealing it."

Swami Ji again smiled and said, "Now, I don't have any specific family as I have renounced all worldly ties. The whole world is my family. You are no way different to me than Sanjana. But I know that she is a wonderful girl with a good understanding of scriptures and a natural talent for composing verses. She can make your deficiency good. May God bless both of you."

Then Bhaskar took leave from him and moved out of his room, but Swami Ji's words were echoing in his ears. *"She can make your deficiency good."* He felt a little embarrassed by the idea that Swami Ji, with his clairvoyance, could notice his feelings for Sanjana. But his words filled Bhaskar's heart with a hue of romantic fancy and happiness. He felt as if Sanjana was made for him, and his destiny had planned their rendezvous. Suddenly, her resplendent beauty flashed before his eyes, and he started praying to God to make him fortunate enough to get Sanjana as his life partner.

The whole ashram staff gathered in the lobby to bid him adieu. Bhaskar thanked all of them individually and proceeded to his return journey. Bhaskar realised that Swami Ji's affection towards him had resulted in special treatment at the ashram. This time, he was relaxed about the route because of the company of the volunteer. He realised that during his upward journey to Tapovan, he was very confident, and later his confidence elevated to a status of overconfidence and threw him into an uncrackable maze of the glacier. However, his overconfidence was purged by the extra miles stamped by him. But he was never so relaxed.

He was enjoying the trek when the volunteer revealed a fact that stunned him again. The volunteer told him that he was trekking for the second time in the same week. His previous journey was to Gangotri, when Swami Ji sent him with a small piece of gold to sell and bring the cash of its value. He did accordingly. This information made Bhaskar realise the exceptional powers of Swami Ji to foresee the future. He couldn't have believed any such incident prior to his meeting with Swami Ji, but now, everything was obvious and needed no evidence.

The Retreat

Bhaskar reached Bhojwasa where Swami Ji's reference given by the volunteer to the manager of the facility helped him acquire a rent-free room in the guest house. The volunteer advised him to stay for the night in the guest house and then proceed to Gangotri the next morning. He thanked the volunteer for guiding him. He also requested the volunteer to communicate his expressions of reverence to Swami Ji and thankfulness to the staff. The volunteer then left for his return journey.

Bhaskar roamed around the place for many hours enjoying the natural beauty of the Himalayan valley until he felt it was too late to remain outside. He reached the guest house, had dinner and went to bed. Now, Bhaskar had some moments of privacy to review the incidents of the last twenty-four hours. He was astounded by experiencing the clairvoyance of Swami Ji. Earlier, he considered it a pseudoscience, but now, the obvious needs no evidence. The lie that Bhaskar told to Swami Ji's family at Gangotri, too, was known to him, but he was not annoyed at his telling a lie. He rather instructed him to tell the truth to Sanjana. Swami Ji's assertion that *"Sanjana can make your deficiency good"* was beyond his understanding, but the statement didn't puzzle him, it rather aroused a distinctive kind of benevolent interest in her. Sanjana's memory filled his heart with a feeling of mystical happiness, and he was lost in her thoughts until he fell asleep.

He woke up in the morning without any hurry. After getting ready for the return, he checked out of the guest house and began his trek to Gangotri. He didn't find any other tourists on the way, but he continued without any difficulty as the trail was clear and comparatively much easier than his previous day's journey. This time, he trekked with ease, admiring the beauty of nature and taking multiple stops. He reached Gangotri around four o'clock in the evening.

He first reached the bus stop where he booked a sleeper berth on the night bus to New Delhi. He knew that this was the only bus that had a sleeper facility. He was relaxed as the ticket was booked and he still had plenty of time. He also had to pick up his belongings from the dormitory where he left his excess baggage while leaving for Tapovan. He wandered around for a while and then reached the dormitory. He rested there for an hour and then left with all his belongings. On the way to the bus stop, he had a light meal. On reaching the bus stop, he found his bus stationed there. He had his bag placed in the luggage compartment and then occupied his berth. In a short while, the bus left, and he fell asleep after saying goodbye to Gangotri and Sanjana.

Reaching the Terminus

Bhaskar reached New Delhi.

He had just alighted from the bus when he found himself surrounded by several taxi drivers offering to take him to a good economy hotel. He handed over his luggage to the taxi driver, who promised to drop him at a good hotel at half the fare. When he asked the taxi driver about the reason for offering a fifty percent discount, he came to know that the hotels pay a good commission to them for bringing customers. He asked the taxi driver to take him to a budget hotel that was clean and tidy.

Within a few minutes, he was at a hotel. The receptionist started telling him about the facilities and amenities of the hotel. Bhaskar was not interested in all that. He found the hotel clean and well managed. So, he paid the taxi fare and finished the formalities of checking in. While making entries in the guest register, he asked about the distance of Birla temple from the hotel and the visiting hours of the temple. The receptionist told him that it would take him a maximum of twenty minutes to reach Birla Temple by taxi and the temple was kept open from 4:30 am to 9:00 pm, except for an hour in the afternoon from 1:30 pm to 2:30 pm. Bhaskar looked at his watch, which showed 8:00 am. The receptionist instructed a servant to carry his luggage and guide him to the room. Bhaskar was in his room in no time.

He quickly climbed into bed as the overnight bus journey had left him jaded and weary. But he was waiting with bated breath to reach the temple. So, he decided to get ready quickly and reach there as soon as possible.

Bhaskar got ready, handed over the key at the reception and moved out of the hotel. He got a taxi and within fifteen minutes, he was at the entrance gate of Birla temple.

The Epiphany

As soon as Bhaskar got out of the taxi, he realised the grandeur of the temple. "Shri Laxmi Narayan Temple" was written on the main gate of the temple. Seeing the temple, Bhaskar felt his heart beating fast. He entered the temple, which was spread over a very large area and the entire campus was filled with natural beauty. Bhaskar realised that the temple was an outstanding specimen of Nagara style architecture. He was overwhelmed by the architecture and beauty of the entire complex, with exquisite fountains, beautiful replicas and sculptures depicting religious and national spirit, murals exhibiting legendary stories of Hindu religion and walls displaying canonical texts.

Bhaskar reached the sanctum sanctorum of the main temple, which was a huge hall that housed the life-like idols of Lord Vishnu and Goddess Lakshmi. He was awed by the extraordinary beauty and attractiveness of the idols that reminded him of the photo in his grandfather's room. He stayed in the temple for time enough to have a complete and careful observation of almost everything in the hall.

He had just exited the hall when he saw a guide addressing a group of visitors and telling them about the height of the peak of the temple. Out of curiosity, he also looked at the peak of the tower of the main temple.

He was taken aback by what he saw. He screamed excitedly, "Oh my God! It is exactly that." His heart started beating faster. He felt the whole world spinning. Bhaskar looked at the ground and wanted to close his eyes. As soon as he closed his eyes, he felt as if hundreds of conch shells were ringing all around. He felt dizzy and found himself too feeble to keep standing. He gathered all his strength and somehow managed to reach the nearby visitor's bench. The structure that had appeared in his dream was before him in reality. He experienced the whole dream appearing before his eyes like a movie. Drops of sweat were rolling down his face and he felt as if he was flying. He had never had such an experience. He got scared lest he would die of cardiac arrest. He closed his eyes and laid on the bench.

After some time, he felt normal and opened his eyes. He was trying to recover his strength that was at the nadir. He took out a handkerchief from his pocket and wiped his face. Then he looked around him, but he didn't see anything unusual. He gathered his courage again and looked towards the top of the temple. This was the same building that used to appear in his dreams. He used to have just a momentary glimpse of the building in his recurrent dream, and it was for this reason that he remained unable to identify the structure.

Now Bhaskar gained control over himself, and his mind started functioning normally too. So, very soon, he realised that the building was exactly the same, but in the dream, he was standing at another location. He tried to pinpoint the location from where he could get the similar angular view of the temple as he had in his dream. He was moving forward, estimating and making his calculations to find the precise location. He reached many points in the premises and observed the peak of the temple from there, but he was not satisfied. He felt as if either he could not recall the dream accurately or could not make some very simple calculations. He felt as if all his abilities had shunned him. But, very soon, he realised that all this havoc was a result of extreme anxiety and emotional turbulence.

He felt disappointed and disgusted. Only then, did he remember his grandfather's catchphrase, *"When things seem out of your control, leave everything to God, without doubt and without thinking about the consequences."*

He decided to forget everything and trust God. He focused his attention on the fact that his grandfather had sponsored his trip and, as per his instructions, he was expected to observe the temple very keenly. That's what he should do first.

Bhaskar had already visited the main temple, so he walked ahead and visited the temples of Lord Krishna, Lord Shankar and Goddess Durga respectively, and observed all the scenery, wall paintings and religious texts with great care and attention. But, neither could he understand anything, nor did he see anything special.

He had a minute observation of all the idols, artefacts and replicas installed in the premises. He had been in the temple premises for about three hours and had seen almost everything. Now he was also looking at the empty walls. And then, he saw an inscription on one of the walls. He started reading it and experienced goosebumps with the initial lines of the text. He quickly read it through and read it again and again. Now he had answers to all his questions. So, this was the place where his grandfather wanted him to reach. This was his grandfather's plan. Now there was no doubt in his mind. The end of all the clutter of almost a month and the key to the answers to all the questions was lying inscribed on a red stone.

The inscription read:

Post Script

On Jyeshtha Shukla 1st Samvat 1998, dated 27th May 1941, at Birla House, New Delhi, Mr. Pt. Krishnapal Sharma made about one Tola gold from one Tola mercury in front of us. The mercury was put in a soapberry nut. A white powder of an unidentifiable herb and a yellow powder, which would hardly be one or one and a half Ratti in weight, were put in the mercury. Then the soapberry nut was closed with clay and then enveloped by two earthen lamps joined with each other and kept on fire. The fire was kept ablaze by continuous air blow for about three quarters of an hour. When the coal started burning to ashes, it was released into the water. Gold poured out from the envelope of lamps. On weighing, the gold was just a Ratti less than a Tola. It was pure gold. We did not know what the secret of the procedure was and what those two powders were. Pandit Krishnapal stood at a distance of ten-fifteen feet from us while carrying out all the activities. At the moment, Mr. Amrutlal V. Thakkar (Prime Minister of Harijan Sevak Sangh), Mr. Goswami Ganesh Dutt Ji Lahore, Secretary of Birla Mill Delhi Mr. Sitaram Khemka, Chief Engineer Mr. Wilson and Viyogi Hari were present. We were all surprised to see the affair. Mr. Seth Jugal Kishore Birla provided us with this opportunity to watch the whole process.

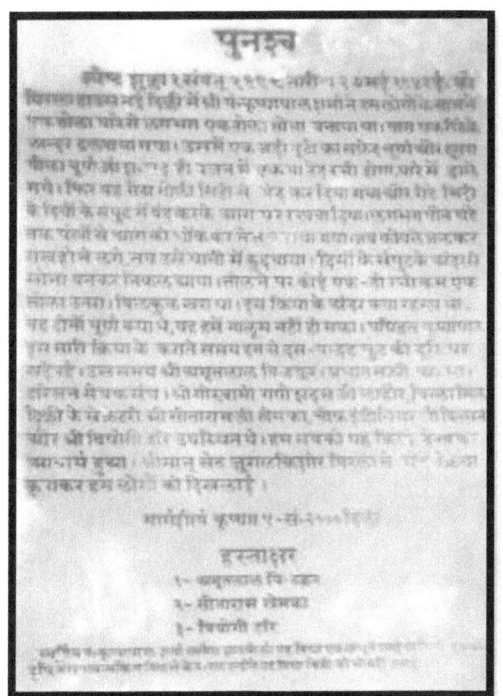

Margshirsh Krishna 5 Samvat 2000 Delhi

Signature

1: Amrutlal V Thakkar   2: Sitaram Khemka   3: Viyogi Hari

Late Pt. Krishnapal Sharma Rasvaidya Shastri learned about this method from an ascetic, but he did not communicate the method to anyone because he could not find a deserving person.

Reading the inscription proved to be an epiphany for Bhaskar. Now everything seemed meaningful to him: a box full of soapberry shells, earthen lamps, a sack of clay, a bottle of mercury and the meticulously packed leather pouches containing yellow and white powders. His grandfather had facilitated everything, even the trivial things, in order to rule out any running about in search of any material. He also realised that his grandfather drafted the letter so brilliantly that even a great scholar like Swami Ji was unable to guess the real message.

Then he remembered that the weight of mercury was seven Ser and, according to the Alchemists' Code of Conduct, an alchemist could sponsor a prodigy up to a maximum of seven Ser of gold. His grandfather had helped him, but he didn't violate any rule of the Alchemists' Code of Conduct. He thought:

'He didn't tell me the method of making gold because I don't know what those powders are. And according to the rules, he could not tell me the secret before attaining the age of thirty years.'

He realised that his grandfather could have planned to endow him with a huge amount of gold directly, but as per the Alchemists' Code of Conduct, his grandfather made him stand the test. Once he cleared the test and fulfilled the criteria, only then was he rewarded. All this setup was just a framework for that ordeal. He felt great admiration for the sacred ideals and norms of his grandfather. Now, Bhaskar understood clearly the reason his grandfather was regarded as a divine figure by people. He considered himself to be fortunate to have been born into his lineage.

Bhaskar looked at the sky and said, "Dada Ji, you have solved all the problems. You did so much just for me. Twenty years ago, you planned and implemented it today. You were exceptional and unique. No, no, let me correct myself. You are exceptional and unique because I can feel your consciousness right now, and I know you are here. I can feel you all around me."

Only then did Bhaskar feel as if someone whispered in his ear to look back. There was no one. Bhaskar looked back and saw the peak of the temple. Now he was standing at the right place. Exactly at the same angle from where he could see the same view of the temple that he had seen in his dream.

Bhaskar felt as if a heavy burden had been lifted from his shoulders. He was very happy to be able to choose the career of his choice. Now there would be no financial problems for him or his family. Now his family would become rich. He would bring gold bangles for his mother and repay all his father's loans.

Bhaskar suddenly felt a tremor of a burning question that arose in his mind. He thought, "Will all this make his father give up his wish for his son to hold an influential government job?" He mulled over it a little. No, never, his father had brought him up and got him educated beyond his financial capabilities. It was his father's sole ambition that his son grabs a lucrative job that offered money, power and recognition. His father could give him permission to do whatever he wanted but couldn't give up the primary desire that fuelled his life. A gloomy uneasiness enveloped Bhaskar's heart and mind. He felt as if everything he had received had turned useless and all his toil was in vain.

He forgot the benefactions he had received just now. He felt that his meetings with learned spiritual saints and scholars like Cave Baba, Shastri Ji, the alchemist and Swami Ji were futile. He thought that it would have been better if he had never met Sanjana. He recalled what Swami Ji told him with great affection about her natural talent for composing verses. He felt anxious, thinking that happiness had suddenly deserted him.

Suddenly, he remembered the same statement that had always proved to be a panacea to his tribulations, *"When things seem out of your control, leave everything to God, without doubt and without thinking about the consequences."* He tried to focus his attention on praying to God to transform his father's opinion. But he found it very difficult to even imagine that his father could give up his stubborn desire. He again affirmed that it was better to leave everything to God without any doubt and without worrying about the result. He consoled himself by assuring himself that every time he had left the situation at the mercy of God, he had received miraculous results. In the forest while searching for Shastri Ji, and in the glacier when he lost his way, every time the mercy of God showered on him. However, doubts were still flickering in his mind, but he dismissed them firmly.

He reiterated that, *"If something is left to God, then there is no need to think about it, nor about its possible consequences. Whatever God does, it is for good."*

To divert his attention from these perplexing thoughts, Bhaskar tried to think of something else. Only then did he remember that he had a sealed letter from his grandfather, and he was very curious to read it. But among all these hectic events, he had forgotten the letter. He sat on a nearby bench and opened the envelope.

The letter read:

Dear Bhaskar,

If you are reading this letter, you have already found what I kept for you as my blessing. It will enable you to pursue your interests and it will be more than enough for you to eradicate the financial problems of your family and provide you with favourable conditions to let your talent grow and bloom to perfection. You can spend it as you wish because you acquired it by proving your abilities.

You should understand that your father has great love and affection for you. But his perception of a happy life is different from that of mine. However, he cannot be blamed for his perception. He remained deprived of the basic amenities and facilities till his youth and it was my fault for ignoring the concerns of a child and an adolescent mind. A prolonged deprivation made him a rebel against the way of life I pursued.

His experiences paved the way to materialise and realise all his unfulfilled yearnings through you. His perception has turned so strong that it is impossible to persuade him through communication. He will never agree to parley with a follower of my philosophy of life, as he considers my way to be leading to poverty, deprivation and destitution. He will not, anyhow, shun his ambitions for you until he witnesses the similar results from an alternate pursuit.

Thus, I perceive that your journey starting from your grandfather's room to various places and then culminating in the same room will prove to be an enchanting experience.

You are a wonderful storyteller. Don't you think that the whole set of internal experiences you underwent, the lessons and learnings along with the settings of the events at various places is a befitting plot for your first work? Once you reach home, sit in solitude and recollect all your thoughts, experiences, events, impressions and learnings. Then pen them down to compose your first work. This is what you are already good at.

Weave all your experiences as an interesting story. I hope your talent and knack for writing will result in a grand success. And a demonstration of your talent to create early success will be the only way to win your father's favour to pursue a different area of interest. Once he realises that there are many fields to work which may bring similar or rather better achievements, I think he will easily agree with you.

Remember, the world does not support strugglers, rather shoves them to fall. You need to demonstrate your capabilities and prove your worth, and then you will be honoured, loved and welcome.

Lastly, what you have received is not a grace or favour for being my grandson. I would rather declare you to be my intellectual heir without considering your birth, caste, age and lineage, because I think your shoulders are strong enough to carry our heritage safely and your intellect is bright enough to enhance its glory.

With blessings,
Pushkar Dixit

Bhaskar's vision got blurred as tears rolled down his eyes. He was extremely emotional, feeling the affection and care that his grandfather had for him. He also felt proud of his grandfather. He was astounded by the plan that his grandfather had made and executed. He realised and admitted the exceptional abilities that his grandfather possessed, which revealed only a split part of the heritage of great Indian masters.

Bhaskar realised that it was a master plan that enabled him to achieve his destiny. He was just a character who acted as per the assigned role, and everything came to him as a fortuity. He didn't do anything, except move from one place to the other. Then he realised that the whole plot was so well-knit that there was no room for any further action on his part. It was just because of this that he was able to meet exceptional personalities like Shastri Ji, the Alchemist, the Aghori ascetic, Swami Ji and Sanjana. Bhaskar realised that all the problems and difficulties of his life had been abolished, and now he had another task: grab his destiny, which would be a cakewalk for him with all the support provided by his grandfather. Suddenly, he recalled what Shastri Ji had said to him. *"Your grandfather has designed your destiny."* Bhaskar fully agreed to the statement.

Bhaskar realised that the most valuable gift that he received was the affirmation of the genuineness of the exceptional achievements of the ancient Indian tradition of knowledge, and not the amount of gold he would possess. He recalled numerous incidents when he came across several people who declared them as rational and labelled the Indian tradition of knowledge as a collection of pseudosciences. On many occasions, he himself doubted the Indian approach towards various branches of study. Actually, the achievements of Indian scholars were exceptionally ahead of their time and thus, they were too scholarly to be comprehended by the masses. So, those great masters, in order to ensure compliance, transformed the concepts into religious and social practices. Later, the practices got distorted and deviated from the basic purpose, and, with the passage of time, turned into totally different customs. Now, Bhaskar felt that his vision was turning clearer, and he was gaining an insight to comprehend those glorious achievements of the past, spontaneously. He remembered what Cave Baba said, *"Science cannot transcend senses and language cannot express silence."* He agreed with it, and firmly believed that all the great Indian masters triumphed in the knowledge that transcended human limits.

The culmination of all his efforts made him ecstatic and so he was on cloud nine, but his feet were firm on the ground. He made a commitment to himself that he would devote his life to the purpose of restoration of the glory of ancient Indian knowledge, which was ages ahead of the achievements of contemporary societies.

He was floating in the ocean of emotions and feelings until a security guard approached him and requested him to leave the premises as the temple was to be closed for an hour. Bhaskar kept the letter in his pocket and walked to the main gate with a thought.

"Sanjana, I will come to you soon."

About the Author

S. P. Nayak

S. P. Nayak works as a senior faculty member in the faculty of Communication Skills with Government Polytechnic College, Nowgong under the Department of Technical Education, Government of Madhya Pradesh. He is a Gold Medalist in his post graduation in English Literature from Jiwaji University, Gwalior. He also holds Cambridge TKT certification for faculty members. Having experience of more than fourteen years in Academics, he has been associated with many organisations like ICFAI, Max New York Life etc. at various places in the capacities of Soft Skills Trainer, Training Manager and Placement Coordinator. He has been a frequent contributor to *The Times of India* and *The Wire*.

www.ingramcontent.com/pod-product-compliance
Lightning Source LLC
LaVergne TN
LVHW041608070526
838199LV00052B/3034